Edward White, Samuel Minton, James Baldwin Brown

Life and Death

A reply to the Rev. J. Baldwin Brown's Lectures on Conditional Immortality

Edward White, Samuel Minton, James Baldwin Brown

Life and Death

A reply to the Rev. J. Baldwin Brown's Lectures on Conditional Immortality

ISBN/EAN: 9783337142155

Printed in Europe, USA, Canada, Australia, Japan

Cover: Foto ©Andreas Hilbeck / pixelio.de

More available books at **www.hansebooks.com**

LIFE AND DEATH.

A REPLY TO THE REV. J. BALDWIN BROWN'S LECTURES
ON CONDITIONAL IMMORTALITY.

BY THE

REV. EDWARD WHITE,

MINISTER OF ST. PAUL'S CHAPEL, HAWLEY ROAD, KENTISH TOWN.

WITH

THREE LETTERS ON THE SAME SUBJECT,

BY THE

REV. SAMUEL MINTON, M.A.,

LATE MINISTER OF EATON CHAPEL.

Reprinted from the "Christian World."

LONDON:

ELLIOT STOCK, 62, PATERNOSTER ROW.

1877.

PREFACE.

In the spring of the present year the Rev. J. Baldwin Brown, B.A., of Brixton, delivered four lectures at his own Church against the doctrine of Conditional Immortality. These were reported in the *Christian World*, a weekly periodical which claims a circulation of one hundred and thirty thousand copies. The following letters, by the courtesy of the Editor, appeared in the same serial. And inasmuch as they offer a brief explanation of the leading doctrines taught by those who hold to the faith that man owes his immortal life not to descent from Adam, but to Redemption, and at the same time deal with the principal objections made to that faith by popular preachers, it has been thought well to reprint them in a more permanent form as a manual for inquirers.

E. W.

Brathay House, Tufnell Park, N.
       June, 1877.

CONTENTS.

LIFE AND DEATH.

———◆———

LETTER I.

SIR,—In offering a few comments on Mr. Baldwin Brown's lectures against Conditional Immortality, I must first of all thank him for devoting his energies to a subject avoided by the general public. We, who have for many years set forth the arguments by which that doctrine is sustained, had become so accustomed to our lack of success in breaking the silence of the leading preachers of the Gospel, that it seemed almost wonderful when a man in Mr. Brown's position showed signs of comprehending the breadth and the gravity of the questions raised, and undertook to canvass the quality of our endeavours. Mr. Brown's passionate hostility to this doctrine is so much more rational, manly, and even Christian, than the persistent dumbness and indifference of the generality of preachers, that the public owes a debt of gratitude to one who at least discerns the issues at stake, and courageously acknowledges that there is a case which deserves serious consideration. Such a course is all the more meritorious if, as the lecturer tells us, much of the printed matter put forth by sundry advocates of that doctrine is of ghastly dulness, and has proved a weariness to his flesh. I know of no excuses for the existence of such literature except these two : first, that every considerable movement in theology has in past ages been accompanied by a flood of pamphlets and articles which would be very painful reading to a modern lecturer ; and, secondly, that Providence seems to avenge the steady refusal of the ablest writers to handle these questions, by permitting the literary activity of less eloquent brethren, who, if not so learned or brilliant, are often much more seriously in earnest than their superiors. But genuine love for truth will lead us not to be ashamed even of the most illiterate endeavours to extend its sovereignty in the world. Courageous faith also prompts us to sympathy with all who share it, even if their dialect be Galilean, and their argument now and then a little paradoxical. Yet Mr. Baldwin Brown will not forget, while honouring a few of us beyond our deserts with so distinguished a share of his attention, that on the same side are a multitude of other writers, ancient and modern, Asiatic, European, and American, whose learning and capacity it would be impertinent alike for me to extol or for him to depreciate.

THE DOCTRINE TAUGHT BY THE EARLY CHRISTIANS.

1. This doctrine is taught, as plainly as possible, by writers whose close relation with the apostles gives the utmost weight to their remarkable words. Irenæus, the scholar of Polycarp, who was the disciple of St. John, teaches that "Life is not from ourselves. nor from our nature ; but is given or bestowed according to the grace of God ; and, therefore, he who preserves this gift of life, and returns thanks to Him who bestows it, shall receive 'length of days for ever and ever.' But he who rejects it, and proves unthankful to his Maker for creating him, deprives himself of the gift of duration to all eternity ; *ipse se privat in seculum seculi perseverantiâ.*" "For," he adds

in his third book, " it was for this end that the Word of God was made man, and He who was the Son of God became the son of man, that man, having been taken into the Word, and receiving sonship, might become the son of God. For by no other means could we have attained to incorruptibility, unless we had been united to Incorruptibility and Immortality. But how could we be joined to incorruptibility and immortality unless first Incorruptibility and Immortality had become that which we also are, so that the corruptible might be swallowed up by incorruptibility, and the mortal by immortality?"

In the very same manner Athanasius, even so late as the year A.D. 360, speaks of the object of the Incarnation in his striking treatise on the Incarnation of the Word. " For the transgression of the command brought men back to their natural condition : so that, even as when not existing they had been created, so also they should undergo destruction of being in the course of time. And justly ; for if possessing the nature of not being once, by the presence and philanthropy of the Logos they were called into being, it was right that men, being emptied of the knowledge of God, and turning to the things that are not, (for evil things are things that are not, but good things really are, since they proceed from the really existing God,) should be emptied also of eternal being, and this is for them, being dissolved, to remain in death or extinction. For man is according to nature mortal, as a being who has been made out of things that are not. But on account of his likeness to God he could by piety ward off his natural mortality, and remain indestructible if he retained the knowledge of God, or lose his incorruptibility if he lost his life in God." A doctrine, then, which has at least the sanction of the remotest Christian antiquity—which has a number of times since been revived and set forth against prevailing error—until at length it has been illustrated by the genius of Dr. Rothe, by the profound learning of Professor Hudson, of Cambridge, U.S.A., in his work on " Debt and

Grace," which makes all other writings on the subject seem almost illiterate, and at last by the vigorous logic and spiritual energy of Mr. Dale,—such a doctrine can scarcely be treated with contumely as a speciality of modern theorists, of puny literalists, or " brutal " materialists.

MR. BALDWIN BROWN'S SEVERITY.

2. And this leads me to acknowledge that a certain difficulty attends the endeavour to present these reflections on the recent lectures to your readers—the difficulty, I mean, which arises from the tone into which Mr. Baldwin Brown has allowed himself to descend in his treatment of the "school " to which he is opposed. Conceding at the outset that he has to do with " a band of most sincere and earnest Christian thinkers," he has afterwards qualified that concession by so many imputations of " bitterness," " hardness," " coldness," " blindness," " Pharisaism," and other bad characteristics which I do not care to repeat, that it is by no means easy to reply with decorum to such an adversary. Nevertheless it must be done, and done without retaliation, or mingling of personal vindication with the prosecution of so lofty an argument. One consideration only I will submit to Mr. Brown in this regard. He will on reflection admit that the tone of "judicial calmness " and fairness, which he extols as the proper attribute of a scientific man of the first class—the temper, for example, which Professor Huxley would certainly exhibit in any controversy with Dr. Elam or Mr. Carruthers on the doctrine of Evolution which these physiologists deny— is pre-eminently the tone and the temper which become those who believe their opponents to be "sincere and earnest Christian thinkers "; and that the discovery of truth is only hindered by language which provokes the susceptibilities of the persons whom he seeks to persuade, and is justified neither by the example of good writers in other departments of inquiry, nor by any manifest disparity of intelligence in the two parties

to the present discussion. It is a needless demand on time to be required to prove that the maintainers of Conditional Immortality are entitled to respectful treatment.

The main cause now advocated assuredly does not depend on the specialities or minor advances of any single writer ; we form no " school," for I am only one of many who, with various powers, some far greater than any to which I can lay claim, are studying these problems of life and death eternal. We are a scattered company of tentative inquirers into nature and Scripture, ready for all needful changes and amendments as the evidence appears. Strongly united in some leading lines of thought, we differ in detail among our-selves as much as do all bands of explorers in somewhat unknown ground. To throw in our faces our early mistakes seems very hard, especially when this is done by men who, until lately, were confessedly in the dark themselves. We really are willing to learn from friends and foes, and to abandon our errors. But meanwhile give us gentler treatment. Grapple with *the facts*, and help us to understand them. Do not visit us with so much unmerciful castigation. It is only Balaam who smites the willing Ass, refusing to advance farther, and brought to a stand in the road, by the sight of the . Angel with the flaming sword of eternal justice drawn in his hand.

THE DOCTRINE OF INTERPRETATION.

3. I gladly leave this painful topic. There is too much to admire in Mr. Brown to permit of serious grievance. Let us now turn to the real question, in which your readers will be interested far more deeply than in any matters of style debated between theological writers. Underlying the whole structure of Mr. Brown's argument there is a doctrine of interpretation, taking that work in the widest sense, which requires more discussion than he has bestowed on it, since on its validity

depends the whole tremendous issue of this controversy. I
refer to Mr. Brown's method of dealing with facts in nature,
and with the letter of Scripture, in conformity with what he
supposes to be the dictate of some inward inspiration in the
soul of man.

SCRIPTURE MUST DECIDE.

Our doctrine is founded upon the assumption that the
sacred Scripture, taken as a whole, and taken in the most
natural and obvious sense of its main current of expressions,
must determine, as of Divine Authority, our faith on these
questions relating to man's nature and destiny. It is not that
we rest on the supposed meaning of one or two words only,
such as *death* and *destruction*, but that on the twofold issues
of human life hereafter the writers of the whole Bible—a
succession of prophets extending through 1,500 years—are
habitually silent on subjects on which, if natural immortality
be true, they ought to speak ; and as habitually employ terms,
alike in Hebrew and Greek, which exhaust the resources of
both languages in their natural and obvious sense to represent
the object of redemption to be, to confer immortal life on
creatures destitute of immortality, and the result of judgment
to be, the utter destruction of the unsaved. They are
absolutely *silent* on the inalienable immortality of the soul in
the account of man's original creation. They are equally
silent as to any endless result of suffering in a future state as
involved in the original threat of death to Adam in Paradise,
or descending upon his posterity. They are *silent* from one
end of Scripture to the other as to man's inherent possession
of the transcendent attribute of a God-like eternity. This
alleged underlying faith or instinctive knowledge never once
breaks out into strains similar to those of Mr. Brown's second
lecture. All we get even from Isaiah's "hallowed lips,"
touched with a divine fire, is an exhortation to " Cease from
man whose breath is in his nostrils, for wherein is he to be

accounted of?" There is the same noteworthy *silence* in the law of Moses, which entered "that the offence might abound," that "sin" might be "known"; the place beyond all others where the penalty of the endless suffering of a condemned immortal ought surely to have appeared. The Scripture "spake nothing" concerning this doom of the deathless sinner. I invite Mr. Baldwin Brown to maintain a similar silence. If this inward conviction of which he speaks, the result of a Divine inspiration, of our possession by nature, not merely of a spirit which survives in death, but of an *immortal* soul, be so deeply fixed, and so universal—whence the necessity of all this eloquence to maintain the belief among men? Why not be contented, like all the prophets and apostles, with observing a similar dumbness? Nature surely will suffice to teach us to-day the true basis of Christian theology, and to repel the perverseness of four hundred and eighty millions of Buddhists on the other side of the globe, who know as little of natural immortality as Mr. Brown's English friends the "miserable annihilationists."

THE SILENCE AND THE SPEECH OF SCRIPTURE AGREE IN ONE.

But this silence sets forth only half the case. For on the positive side there is to be noted that in treating of the destinies of mankind there run through the Scriptures two broad lines or currents of language, which taken in their most obvious and natural signification teach us that it is the very object of the Incarnation to "give eternal life" to a race which has lost that prospect through sin; while the penalty of impenitence and unbelief will be to incur the aggravated execution of the sentence of destruction which hung over humanity in consequence of its original transgression. For a full representation of the elaborate precision of these two lines of language on life eternal and on the threatened death of sinners, I must refer to my recent volume, where it will be found tabulated in both Hebrew and Greek, and carefully examined both from within and with-

out.   The fullest and most decisive representation ot it is
found in the Gospel of John, to the argument on which I
invite Mr. Brown's particular attention.*   I will only say here
that it is an argument which is every day carrying the judgment
of some sound scholar, and of numbers of educated common-
sense Christians, who read their Bibles with an eye unblinded
by traditional metaphysics.   And no wonder ; for when Mr.
Brown, in these wonderfully vigorous lectures, wishes to hit us
the hardest blows he can, he has *no words*, in all his wide
repertory, wherewith to demolish the doctrine that life eternal,
deliverance from destruction, depends on the Incarnation,
through Regeneration, except the very words which are used
everywhere in the Bible to denote, he says, quite another doctrine.   He speaks of "immortality," but that is only Latin for
not *dying*, in the sense of not *ceasing to be*.   He takes, therefore, this sense of the word, when it suits his theory, but
forbids us to take it anywhere else.   This is just like Mr.
Spurgeon, who says that the words "the worm *dieth* not"
prove that the sinner will "never die—" forgetting that, in order
to make out his case, he takes the word *dieth* in the sense
which he forbids to ourselves in all the rest of the Scripture.
Mr. Spurgeon and Mr. Baldwin Brown must settle this matter
between themselves, and try to arrange some common vocabulary to describe the doctrine condemned, in which they shall
not use *in our sense* the words of the Bible on which they are
attempting to fasten two different interpretations.

4. Now, the result of our studies on human nature, assisted
by the light of modern science, is such as to lead us to find
nothing in humanity that contradicts the action of Omnipotent
Justice and Mercy, so plainly asserted in the Bible, in determining its doom.   The lecturer's wonderful descriptions of man's
glory as an immortal have first been stolen from Christ and
Christianity, and then placed to the account of man by nature.

---

* See a criticism on John vi. at the close of these letters.

But when we look with our recent biologists into the facts of man's individual origin, as they appear before our senses, there is no room left for this astounding theory of a human life endowed with God's own attribute of endless being. Whether Mr. Brown finds it "degrading" and "brutalising" or not, the fact is that human beings originate in processes so precisely analogous to those in which all the rest of the earth's living creation originates, that this romance of indefeasible immortality seems absolutely ludicrous in its pretension. As Mr. Minton puts it, with immense force, "To pronounce it a degradation to humanity for any single human germ which reaches some undefined point of development not to live as long as the Creator is surely the *ne plus ultra* of human self-exaltation." The reader must think out the meaning of these weighty and significant words. Mr. Brown will assist us, as also Professor Huxley and Dr. Maudsley, by telling us *at about what stage of development* this natural and Godlike eternity of man's soul, in his judgment, begins. For our parts we discover nothing in the facts of human origin which contradicts or throws doubt on the proposal to take the language of the Bible just as we find it.

WORD-MONGERING.

5. But Mr. Baldwin Brown treats this proposal of ours to submit our faith to what he calls the "letter" of Scripture with supreme contempt. In these lectures he has exhausted the vocabulary of civilised theological vituperation in setting forth the ignominious quality of the minds who consent to be landed in such conclusions from such premisses. "Word-mongering" is the lightest offence laid to our charge. He insists on our taking as a first principle of interpretation, both in nature and revelation, his magnificent speculation on the inherent immortality of the soul. In compliance with this he calls upon us to deny our very senses in contemplating the origin of the individual human being, and all the laws of

philology in the interpretation of the Bible. Now this style of handling the subject I protest against as wholly inadmissible. Wrong we still may be, but the argument for Conditional Immortality founded on interpretation of the Sacred Scriptures cannot be flipped aside by unworthy nicknames any longer. According to the unanimous judgment of all scholars worthy of the name who have considered the subject, that argument must now be accepted, or seriously answered. A "monger" is only a dealer. A word-monger must be a dealer with words. What else should a man deal with, whose business it is to interpret the records of a Divine Revelation, except the *ipsissima verba* of the sacred Scriptures? To deal with them is to interpret them, to "give the sense," like those old word-mongers Ezra and his compeers. Does it deserve to be called "word-mongering" if I spend a portion of my life in trying to ascertain which of the two modes of interpreting the long lines of words above referred to is the right one, that recommended to me by Mr. Brown's excellent neighbour, Mr. Spurgeon, or that recommended to me by Mr. Baldwin Brown himself—the one holding me up to public reproof, if I do not take his word for it, that "destruction" throughout the Bible signifies "endless misery"—the other pouring on me more philosophical ignominy, if I do not see that the threat of "destruction" signifies the end of sin, and the certainty of final salvation? Is it word-mongering to ask whether in all probability *both* of our advisers on the Surrey side of the Thames are not mistaken ; and whether the language of the Bible ought not to be taken here, as elsewhere in relation to the most important topics, in the "plain grammatical sense" of the terms? Is there any more rational way of spending one's life than in trying to understand the Almighty Spirit, who "spake by the prophets,"—especially when incited to do so by hearing from two honoured friends of mine such contradictory figurative interpretations as these? Is there any obvious absurdity in the proposition to take these two great streams of biblical language in their simplest intention; and thence to infer that the Divine Being designs a deathless life for the righteous alone? It is intolerable to be answered on such a subject, and under such conditions, by contemptuous phrases, which, if they mean anything, mean that we deserve to be numbered for our pains with the lowest of the materialistic crew. It is time for this affectation of superior sense and insight to be laid aside; and for a "learned looking" criticism to be met by its only proper antidote—not a burst of bold assertion, of Platonic poetry, and of confusing eloquence—but by a criticism which is *more* learned, *more* historical, and *more* consonant with the facts of human existence. To that we will bow, but to nothing else; for to yield to aught else seems to us to be tantamount to connivance at "wresting" the Scriptures,— those Holy Scriptures which alone seal to man the promise of the Resurrection to Life Eternal. Mr. Baldwin Brown himself knows nothing for certain of any future state for man apart from those Scriptures; and the least we can do is to strive to the utmost to study the meaning of that "Word which shall judge us at the last day."

A HYPOTHETICAL CONCESSION.

6. I have dwelt on this matter of interpretation first of all, for the knot of the whole debate is here. Apart from the Divine Revelation, Mr. Brown's way of looking at humanity, as possessed of a God-like durability of endless being, is, whether it can be proved or not, undoubtedly the more attractive. I felt, in reading his first lecture, thrilled and delighted with the description of so sublime a destiny for all human beings, and only lamented that the countless hordes of Buddhists and savages whom the earth has bred have thought so differently on their nature and end. If there be no Revelation from God, Mr. Brown is more than welcome to his admirable speculations. Amidst the infinite darkness the best thing that man can then do is to think with Plato, even

if he must die as Harriet Martineau and the evolutionists suppose he will die. But to us the question of interest is, What does the Bible teach? The doctrine of an immortality, acquired by redemption only, is tenable exclusively on a revealed basis. No man who does not first believe in something divine will believe in this. We have no great hope of converting to the doctrine any except serious thinkers and truth-seekers. Mr. Brown's appeals against us to the general public (including all ungodly men who would be assured of safety) are certain of success—with that public. To "spiritual" persons who believe in Christ, however, the question will recur, What does the Bible intend by eternal life and eternal destruction? We are "nowhere" in the theological world if we have not a solid basis in Revelation. It is not, as Mr. Brown repeats *ad nauseam*, that we weakly suppose we glorify God's grace by a ruthless dishonouring of humanity. It is that we think we take the measure of humanity from the testimony of its Maker, and read its destiny in the pages of His message to the world.

We are placed in this difficulty: we have to choose between the lofty speculations of Mr. Brown respecting human nature as such, and the far less exalted statements of the apostles and prophets. It seems to us impossible to reconcile the two. Mr. Brown, like Dr. South, has drawn for us, with a splendid astronomical background, a striking picture of Adam in Paradise, and of the constitutional place of humanity in the great universe. Man was created unconditionally in the image of God, and this includes God's eternity. This transcendent attribute of endless being has never been lost, can never be lost. Well, such is the realistic turn of my mind that, in reading Mr. Brown's almost enthusiastic eloquence on this head, I wished he could have been permitted to deliver that lecture to Adam and Eve, under the shadow of the forbidden tree in Eden, surrounded by their animal associates; congratulating them on this Godlike eternity of theirs, this immortality, or deathlessness, which, in its utmost essence, no sentence of justice should ever dissolve. I fancy that while *they* would have been sorely puzzled by the glorious flights of their distinguished descendant, there would have been at least one delighted auditor of the discourse—and that is the Old Serpent—who would have chimed in at once, at every climax, with a confirmation of the promise that they "should not surely die," since God knew well that in the day in which they ate of the fruit " their eyes would be opened," and they would become Divine in a double sense, being Godlike already in an eternal nature, and Godlike afterwards in an added power of understanding and contradicting the hollow threats of the tyrannical Divinity. But even after hearing the lecture, it would still have remained for the transgressors to be expelled from "the Tree of Life." "Now lest he put forth his hand and take of the tree of life, *and eat and live for ever*—so He drove out the man," saying, " Dust thou art, and unto dust thou shalt return." This may be perhaps consistent with all that the lecturer tells us of Adam's constitution, but, at least, on the surface, it is more confirmatory of the belief of those who say that man was not created, either in body or soul, possessed of indefeasible immortality.

MR. BROWN'S LEADING MISTAKE.

7. But this leads me to observe that Mr. Brown has been throughout singularly inequitable in misrepresenting our opinion as to man's relation to the animals. Because we have insisted much on the reality of that relation on one side— on the obvious organic similarity between man and the higher animal races—a fragmentary truth to which great attention is drawn by modern biology—we have been charged with holding the most degrading and " brutalizing " views of man's nature as a whole. Because we have insisted that man's foundation is in the dust, we are set forth as denying or almost ignoring his relations with the Spiritual, the Infinite, the Eternal. Now,

instead of expending a great deal of your valuable space in indignant repudiation of these inexcusable imputations, I shall just give one quotation from *Life in Christ* which will dis· pose at a stroke of this whole fabric of well-intended rhetorical calumny.   This shall be taken from the fourth chapter, where I am summing up what may be probably determined by science *before consulting revelation ;* and the result is as follows :— " Whether therefore we consider man's power of speech, his moral nature, his capacity for religion and worship, or his capacity for indefinite progression, we are led to the same probable conclusion, on purely scientific grounds, that this creature, though often sunk into the deepest depths of barbarism, so as to approximate towards the animals in the methods and ends of life to a degree which almost abolishes the human sense of superiority to them, was a distinct creation of the Infinite Power, and has not grown out of the next order of *primates* beneath him by a natural evolution. A ' beast's heart' was not given to him at his origin " (p. 38).   It is not likely that the pen which wrote thus of human nature, contemplated under the light of nature only, has written anything of the character of a debasing materialism respecting it afterwards, when interpreting a Divine Record which begins by declaring that "God made man in His own image."

Mr. Brown may be assured that he has wrought conspicuous injustice by his elaborate attempts to represent us as looking upon man as a beast, because we hold that the lofty, Godlike human nature came under sentence of death for sin.   If man had been created an archangel, he might still have incurred death for sin, without losing in his fall the archangelic nature. Just so we hold that man lost the right to the tree of life, without losing the intrinsic Godlikeness of his moral being.   When Mr. Brown says that the Incarnation implies the eternity of this Godlike nature, we reply that this is the very question in dispute.   We say (relying on the Scriptures) that the object of Incarnation was to communicate eternal life to the Godlike nature which had lost it.

I cannot do better than end this already too extended letter by citing, with perfect assent, the words of Mr. Dale, when dealing lately at my church with this hideous misrepresentation of our faith. "The tree of life was no graceful ornament of the Paradise of God; it was there because man needed it; it is the immortal symbol of the truth that there are wants in human nature which only a Divine life can satisfy, possibilities which only a Divine life can fulfil. A beast! No! Man is infinitely more than that. It is not a beast who struggles vainly against destiny in the ancient tragedy. It is not a beast that in modern times resents with infinite sorrow and fierce revolt the pain and disorder which have come on this creation. It is not a beast that has sought for gods to worship in the stars of heaven, and in the meanest and most majestic objects on earth, in the clouds, in the winds, and in the heroic founders of national communities. It is not to a beast that the moral law appeals. It is not to a beast that the life of God can be given. It is not a beast that has the power to refuse it." After this, I hope we shall hear no more of Mr. Brown's unbefitting accusations. The greatness of man is implied in the very words of the awful curse on abandoned sinners: "These, as natural, irrational creatures, made for capture and extinction, speak evil of the things which they understand not, and shall utterly perish in their own corruption (2 Peter ii. 12).

In my next letter I shall treat of Mr. Brown's opinion that there are no moral differences between men corresponding with the idea of an eternal distinction in their destinies.

LETTER II.

A CONSIDERABLE section of Mr. Baldwin Brown's recent lectures treats of principles in which there is no difference of opinion between us.

A larger portion of them consists of argument based on representations of the doctrine of Conditional Immortality, for which I do not acknowledge any responsibility. Possibly such representations are justified by the materialistic theories and incautious language of other writers, and I leave them to make their own defence against their formidable assailant, if any defence be available. Other portions of Mr. Brown's lectures proceed on a remarkable and total disregard of the carefully graduated language of assent and conviction variously applied by me to the long succession of propositions comprised in the volume which he has honoured by so much observation. Conclusions, which are there set forth only as probabilities, liable to much reasonable question, are cited and dealt with by the lecturer as essential and tenaciously-held portions of the main argument. I may instance the argument on judgment by "fire." Single sentences even are held up to ridicule or reprobation, detached from a long context which greatly and purposely qualifies their strength of tone. I have no remedy against this ordinary misfortune of theological writers, except time and the gradual increase of patience and information in our opponents. If I have learned nothing else by prolonged study of these controversies, I have at least learned to entertain beliefs, on different branches of the subject, under very different measures of certitude, and to express them with corresponding degrees of confidence as to the weight of the evidence by which such beliefs are supported. Your readers would not be edified by any comments which might be suggested by those sections of Mr. Brown's discourses which have been occasioned by some considerable inattention to these lights and shades of conviction and expression. It will better satisfy the public interest if I forego all minor personal vindication, and restrict these defensive comments to the points on which Mr. Brown has concentrated the chief force of his attack. Our opponents, so much divided in their own solution of the mystery of the past and future, are more powerful in assault on isolated details of the doctrine of Immortality in Christ alone, than on the *tout ensemble* of the leading argument; and are far stronger in the siege laid against us, than in the work of constructing a coherent and credible theology which may explode and replace our alleged delusions.

MR. BROWN'S FIRST OBJECTION.

The effect of Mr. Brown's lectures depends principally on two chief objections; if these can be satisfactorily encountered I imagine that even his antagonism might undergo some considerable diminution. It gives me sincere pleasure to acknowledge that the first of these objections could have been felt so deeply only by a noble and sympathetic intelligence, and could have been expressed so eloquently only by one whose words deserve the most careful consideration. I shrink from the risk of damaging the force of Mr. Brown's argument by translating it into my own language. But full citation would involve the reproduction of nearly half these discourses, and therefore I will endeavour to state fairly, if briefly, the drift of the reasoning.

It is said, then, that in affirming "our doctrine" of Regeneration unto Life we are asserting nothing less than an infinite and generic distinction between two classes of mankind, the mortal and the immortal, for which no sufficient justification is discoverable in their nature or character while on earth. We have contended that in the original lapse of man he fell from the enjoyment of God's favour, and the prospect of immortality, back into the condition of an evanescent ephemeron, absolutely doomed to perish utterly ; so that it is through redemption only that any man can now pass into immortality. This transition we have attributed in its direct cause to the Incarnation of the Eternal Word, the Divine Life in the Son of God ; and, in its immediate effect, to the action of the Holy Spirit descending to dwell in the breast of the regenerate sons of God. The state of a person, so " begotten of God," we have declared to be, according to the Apostles, that of a being who has passed out of the order of the perishable into the order of the imperishable and Divine. " Being begotten again, not of corruptible seed, but of incorruptible, by the Word of God living and remaining : for that all flesh is as grass, and all the glory of man is as the flower of the grass. The grass withered, and the flower fell away ; but the Word of the Lord *endureth for ever.* And this is the Word, which, by the Gospel, is preached unto you " (1 Peter i. 22-5. Corrected text).

Mr. Brown, in passages of memorable splendour and beauty, has assisted the maintainers of this faith to realize the stupendous nature of the change which they suppose to have passed upon those who shall in this sense " find life eternal." For my own part I must confess that I do not envy the constitution of the mind which could read unmoved the thrilling lines in which the transcendent greatness of the change supposed is urged on our reflection and appreciation. If Mr. Brown had written nothing else for which Christendom might thank him, those thanks would be surely due for this attempt to rouse us to apprehend afresh the infinities amidst which we are moving in these disputed questions. Hard, and cold, and callous, as he seems to think us, I can only say that in my own case his lectures have revived, in their most overpowering influences, all the awful hours of long-past thought on human destiny, with which for so many years, by night and day, I have been visited, until faith, as it seemed to grow more solid, only threw a darker shade around me ; for, indeed, the first effect of deeper believing is to create a profounder scepticism, arising from the very infinitude which opens before the eye that gazes firmly on eternity. Too vivid conceptions of eternal things are not desirable in the spiritual life of mankind. Yes, it may well be said to us ; Do you indeed believe that regenerate man passes into endless being, or that true faith carries with it a destiny so different from that of common men, as you would assign to it? Who, that reflects on the community of the human race in all its conditions of temporal existence, on its common origin, on its physical, intellectual, and moral unity, on the historical, and ancestral, and social causes which determine so much that we call character, on the many excellencies of the bad, and on the manifold imperfections of the good—can fail to stumble at first at a doctrine which places the seal of indestructibility on the foreheads of some, and relegates the rest of mankind, with all their virtues, struggles and woes, to the realms of the perishable, and the doom of irremediable destruction ?

OUR SOLE AUTHORITY.

I know of no authority but One sufficiently commanding to compel me to this conclusion, and even that one leaves me still staggering under the weight which it lays upon me ; leaves me still applying myself to maintain its revelations against contradiction with a mind "astonied," like Daniel's, when he looked upon the glories and terrors of the invisible realms. Who, indeed, is sufficient for these things? "For we are unto God a sweet savour of Christ in them that are saved, and in them that perish ; to the one we are the savour of death unto death ; and to the other the savour of life unto life." These, however, I say to myself, were the words of one who "wept" and "trembled" as he taught, and staggered sometimes as we do, yet believed in the teaching of the Spirit, and persisted in his faith that nothing less than *death* and *life everlasting* depended on the issues of man's probation here. But they were also the words of one who had not thrown off the burden of faith by a desperate rush into theories, which, if they help a man to imagine himself "sufficient" to grapple with the facts of life and of destiny, relieve only for a moment, by an artificial light not kindled at "the fountain itself of heavenly radiance," and that soon dies out, leaving the darkness deeper than before.

After a renewed and patient study of the objection proposed in all its strength by Mr. Brown, I am compelled to conclude that the authoritative record of Christ does distinctly affirm, in every form, the infinitely differing characters and dooms of good and evil men, and that the lecturer is shrinking from a burden of thought which is laid upon him by Almighty God Himself. For, in the first place, the spiritual classification of mankind found in the Bible, without one exception, is simply and invariably dualistic. The prophets and apostles speak of the RIGHTEOUS and the WICKED, as of creatures differing in the root-principle of their being. I find not even a trace of the modern mode of regarding humanity, in which men discern only moral shades, and deny the existence of distinct colours in character. This lenient estimate of the evil, and lowering estimate of the good, which makes them all of one blood, united by a moral consanguinity, and in itself so demoralising, is resolutely rejected in the teaching of Christ, appointed to " judge the world in righteousness." In the Old Testament we find everywhere the " righteous and the wicked " only, as a classification exhausting the population of the world. In the New Testament this distinction is re-affirmed and accounted for. Christ Himself asserts a supernatural cause for the distinction, which He treats as generic, and as un- affected by the better qualities of " sinners " or the worse qualities of the good. He declares to Nicodemus that some are " begotten of the flesh " only, others are " begotten of the Spirit." He declares that the latter alone are the " sons of God," and the sole inheritors of the heavenly kingdom. " Except a man be born again he cannot see the kingdom of God." " That which is born of the flesh is flesh." " Verily I say unto you, ye must be born again " (John iii.). His apostles persist in this classification. With St. Peter, some " are born again," others not; some are " the people of God," others not; some are the " righteous," others the " ungodly and sinners " (1 Peter i. 23 ; ii. 10 ; iv. 18). With St. John there is the man who is " born of God," and the man who is not ; the man who " abides in death," and the man who has " passed from death unto life " ; the man who " walks in the light," and the man who " walks in darkness " ; the man in whom " eternal life abides," and the man in whom it does not. There is the " world that knows not God," and there are the " sons of God who know Him " (1 John ii. 5). With St. Paul there is the " soulical," or animal man (*psuchicos*) and the " spiritual man " 1 Cor. ii.); the " old" man and the " new "; the old creature and the " new ;" the " earthly man " and the " heavenly " (1 Cor. xv.); the man who " sows to the flesh," and the man who " sows to the Spirit" (Gal. vi.); the man who " has the spirit of Christ," and the man who " has not," and therefore is " none of His " (Rom. viii.). The favourite Pharisaic threefold partition of mankind into the good, the moderately righteous, and sinners is unsanctioned by the apostles of Christ, much more the quite modern classification, which regards humanity as a unit, with principles of good and evil acting in every man. The Bible maintains throughout the ancient and awful generic distinction between the good and the evil; and the Old Testament ends by declaring that whatever difficulty there may be at present in distinguishing the two, in the end the essential difference will appear. "Then shall ye come back, and discern between the righteous and the wicked, between him who serves the Eternal, and him who serves Him ·not. And the wicked shall be ashes under the soles of your feet in the day that I do this, saith the Lord" (Mal. iii. 18; iv. 3).

MR. BROWN'S DIFFERENCE IS WITH THE BIBLE.

The objection thus set forth with so much confidence by Mr. Brown, against the idea of an eternal distinction in destiny, depending on the faint differences in temper and character, is, as Mr. Dale has briefly affirmed, and I have now shown in detail, really an objection against the plainest declarations of revelation. The believers in conditional immortality are under no special obligation to meet this objection. It may be made equally against the catholic theology of Europe. The objection depends on denying the immutable distinctions of good and evil, in the concrete form of character, and savours of the demoralised *morale* of the atheistic philosophy of our time. Righteousness and wickedness are distinctions of infinite import in the choice of souls. He who unites himself to God belongs to a wholly different *genus* of beings from him who refuses God. He becomes "a partaker of the Divine nature," and will "escape the mortality which is in the world through lust" (2 Peter i. 4).

DIVINE SONSHIP OF UNGODLY MEN DENIED BY CHRIST.

There is, further, a noteworthy peculiarity in the doctrine of Christ and His inspired apostles respecting the " sonship " of ungodly men. An argument insisted on by Universalists of all shades, with the utmost assurance, is, that the fatherhood of God renders it positively incredible that He will either destroy or eternally banish any of the human race who are His sons. An earthly father, it is said, who is wise and good, cannot even be imagined as putting to death one of his own children. Much more, therefore, ought such an act to be disbelieved in relation to the "Father of Spirits." I desire to point it out as an appalling peculiarity of Christ's teaching, that He represents, in the strongest manner, the refusal of God to acknowledge the "sonship" of "sinners," or to allow of the claim that He is their "Father" until they repent. The relation of Father, in the bare sense of Creator, cannot, as a matter of fact, be abolished—"we are all His offspring"— but in every other and higher sense, involving moral relationship and eternal love, it is declared to be non-existent in reference to impenitent men. "If God were your Father, ye would love Me. Ye are of your father, the devil," said Christ to the Pharisees. Through sin men have been disinherited; they are "slaves" of sin and death, not "sons of God." The "adoption of sons" comes only with the "new birth" unto righteousness. God does not acknowledge spiritual fatherhood to those who work evil. "He that made them will have no mercy on them." "They shall have judgment without mercy." We are no more worthy to be called His sons. The Divine Word denominates us "sons of God" only when we have passed from death unto life. The popular argument, therefore, against the destruction of unregenerate men, derived from the fatherhood of God, is drawn from a relationship which, in the case of the rebellious, Christ distinctly disowns.

"The chaff He will burn up with unquenchable fire." I
entreat Mr. Brown to cease his unjust accusations against us,
as hard and unfeeling, in bringing these alarming truths to
public notice, and to discontinue his dangerous encourage-
ment given to impenitence by such fallaciously hopeful representations. The real hardness and cruelty lie with those who
conceal the threatenings of God, and thereby "strengthen the
hands of evil doers" to their own ruin, by promising them
"life and peace," and *that* in the awful name of a Being who
has "sworn" that if they do not repent "TO-DAY" they
shall "not enter into His rest." "Except ye repent, ye shall
all likewise perish." "Now is the day of salvation."

ON THE NATURE OF GERMS.

2. It remains to discuss the second part of this objection,
and to ask whether our incapacity to distinguish or "discern"
in all cases "between the righteous and the wicked" is valid
reason for following Mr. Brown in denying the sufficiency of
the distinction, as a basis for infinite differences in destiny.
Here we are thrown back upon some considerations on the
phenomena of germ-life in general, whence it will appear that
the admitted impossibility of pronouncing upon the generic
distinctions in spiritual characters or states, in many of their
earlier forms, forms no argument against the reality of such
distinctions or their infinite consequences. Mr. Brown has
himself supplied the warning against precipitate judgment on
germs, which is applicable in the case before us. When argu-
ing against a supposed fatal error of ours, in which by mis-
take he attributed to us the belief that mankind is not simply
allied on one side to the animal races, but is distinguishable
from them only by shades of development, he very justly
points out that this undistinguishableness of the germs cannot
be pleaded in support of the identification of the two, since
the obscure germ soon demonstrates its hidden forces, and
asserts in humanity its generic superiority to that of the brute.

" The germs, we are assured, of Newton and of his dog Diamond, are, in their incipient stages, absolutely identical. Yes, to Science. But there is something there which it needs a yet Diviner art, in which the philosopher is the priest, to discern, which makes the one germ inevitably into Newton and the other into a dog."

It needs only to transfer this admirably-stated principle to the realms of spiritual life to meet the objection on which Mr. Brown relies in combating the idea of spiritual distinctions wide enough to warrant eternal differences in their fate. The beginnings of all life are mysterious and invisible; the earlier stages of the development are imperfect and obscure. This is true of the body. It is equally true of the " new creature in Christ." There is nothing which can be said against the un-distinguishableness of generic difference in character which might not be said in relation to the early stages of physical development. The Newton and the Diamond are soon re-vealed; but it might puzzle any power less than Omniscience to discriminate the two until development has occurred. The great lesson of biology is the enlargement of our faith as to the hidden life of elementary organisms. Hear how Dr. Maudsley speaks in his latest work on the " Physiology of Mind."

" Those who may be disposed to think it impossible that such important constitutional differences should exist in so small a compass might reflect with advantage on the various undetect-able conditions which may confessedly exist in the minutest organic matter—as, for example, in the delicate microscopic spermatozoon, or in the intangible virus of a fever. And yet it is from the conjunction of one minute spermatozoon with another that are produced the muscles, vessels, nerves, and brain—of a Socrates or a Cæsar. . . . The single cell united with the single germ, each integrating the qualities of ancestors, gives birth to a new organic product, which, minute as it is, contains in latent forms all the potentialities, and displays actually in evolution many of the qualities, of generations of ancestors, male and female, and furthermore evinces new qualities as a result of the organic combination. There is nothing extravagant in the supposition that a single nerve cell has many potentialities. The exquisite minuteness and consummate delicacy of the operations going on around us in the most intimate recesses of nature are even more striking and wonderful than the vastness and grandeur with which the astronomer is concerned" (p. 120).

When, therefore, Mr. Baldwin Brown undertakes to affirm that differences in spiritual character sufficient to account for diverse everlasting destinies are not discernible, we submit to him, first, that sometimes such failure to discern the infinite difference in character between good and evil men arises not from the obscurity of the phenomena, but from the vast extent of a superficial and deceptive profession of religion, or from the spiritual blindness of the observer; and, secondly, that all physical analogy supports the declaration that in two characters, seemingly alike, there may, nevertheless, be such an essential difference that, as in the cases of Christ's two associates, Judas Iscariot and Peter, both much alike to a careless eye, " one of them is a devil," for whom it would be "better if he had never been born"; one of them is a "natural man," an "earthy man," a man "abiding in death," who has developed only evil qualities, or qualities good simply on the human level; while the other, though as yet much undeveloped, contains a germ of Divine Life, which before long will develope into a form of character "equal to the angels," and "worthy of an endless life." "We know not what we shall be, but we know that when He shall appear we shall be like Him, for we shall see Him as He is."

PRACTICAL EFFECTS OF THE DOCTRINE.

I am not careful to answer the allegations made as to the ill effect on character of the reception by spiritual persons of the doctrine of life eternal in Christ only; or on the " degrading" and "brutalising" influence of this doctrine on general society. Those who have lived for many years among Christians who have heartily and devoutly received this doctrine as Divine are in a better position to form a sound judgment on its effects than those who, by their intolerance, have driven away from their sphere of activity all who maintain it. For myself, I can only testify that, knowing well the quality of the spiritual life produced by the teaching of the orthodox theology, I can trace no evil effect as the result of the teaching of life in Christ, in respect of faith, or hope, or love. Those who receive it are seldom merely speculative thinkers, but serious and earnest Christians—persons to whom, in a practical sense, "to live is Christ"; and the result is certainly not to diminish their love to Him, to whom they think they owe their immortality. I can further assure Mr. Baldwin Brown, and thereby relieve his expressed apprehensions, that I have observed no "brutalising" influences, such as he fears, at work among the people who have been subjected to such teaching in this quarter of London now for a quarter of a century. The average of "suicides" in Camden and Kentish Towns will compare favourably, I think, with the average in Brixton. Those who are foremost in zealous belief in this theological speciality are among the least brutal persons within my rather wide acquaintance. Professor Barrett, moreover, very truly declared a few weeks ago in your columns that not a few men of scientific culture have been saved from gross materialism and atheism as the result of hearing Christ preached as the Messenger of Eternal Life.

Indeed, with truth I should sum up the general conclusion, from my own long experience of the spiritual effect of this way of thinking, by saying that it considerably strengthens popular faith in the Bible as a whole; leads to the wholesome conjoint study of both Nature and Scripture, which are hereby shown to be univocal; explains the necessity and results of the

Incarnation of the Word, of Regeneration, of Union with Christ; and while it exalts and reveals the love of God, enables and incites men to preach "judgment to come" *as if they believed it*, and with the most salutary effects on ungodly men's understandings and consciences. Instead of lowering the tone of spiritual life, the tendency of this doctrine is to exalt it, by showing that it is the direct effect of the Personal Indwelling of the Holy Spirit; and that the union of a good man with an Eternal and Intelligible God is no figure of speech, but the deepest of all ascertained facts. In a word, I have not found one of the evil practical consequences augured by Mr. Brown, and I have discerned several excellent results which he never even hints at. Among others, the temptation is taken away from the people of running into the desperate theory of universalism, which, with Mr. Dale, I think to be the most baseless, and one of the most pernicious, of all theological errors. For it is a mode of thought which destroys the real and infinite distinction between good and evil, by representing their natures as mixed, and their ultimate destinies as homogeneous; and which takes away holy love to God, by first of all extinguishing religious fear. Christ is no longer a Saviour from the wrath to come, but only the late-sent guide of a race already Godlike and immortal, and already, on the whole, good and harmless enough, after a comparatively brief purgatory, to inherit Paradise. This is the result of teaching " the solidarity of the race," in Mr. Brown's sense—a phrase as French as the thought which it fitly conveys (there being no Scriptural term for the idea), and removed, as far as the east is from the west, from the doctrine of the New Testament, which teaches that true Christians alone are "of God," while " the whole world lieth in the wicked one." " And the world [*i.e.* the ungodly world] *passeth away*, and its lust, but he that doeth the will of God *remaineth for ever*" (1 John ii. 17). On Mr. Brown's objection to this Scriptural doctrine, of the " passing away of the world and its lust "—in the retribution of the second death—I will offer some remarks in my next letter; after which there will remain only to consider the alleged tendency to speculative atheism and materialism charged upon this doctrine.

LETTER III.

ON THE DOCTRINE OF FUTURE PUNISHMENT BY DESTRUCTION.

In this letter I am to consider Mr. Baldwin Brown's principal objection to that awful doctrine on Future Punishment, which is held by us partly in subjection to positive revelation, and partly as a necessary inference from the truth that immortality is the destiny of those alone who are made regenerate in Christ.

The doctrine of the second Death, which declares that unless men are born twice they will die twice, is represented in the Divine Revelation amidst " blackness, and darkness, and tempest," like that which covered Mount Sinai at the giving of the Law ; and, therefore, none can break through to gaze into the tremendous abyss of Divine wrath, whence bursts the fire that burns into the midst of heaven. To venture into that thick darkness with a design of exploring, or pretending to expound, the secrets of those doleful shades, on which even the flashes of Divine vengeance throw no light, but rather render darkness visible, be far from us. A certain part of the moral effect of the prospect of judgment to come depends on its mystery. This only we know—that God, by all the voices of His prophets, has declared that amidst that darkness the wicked, under "few" or "many" stripes, shall "utterly perish," and that the ungodly world shall "pass away" (2 Peter ii. 9 ; 1 John ii. 17).

This doctrine on future retribution is but a segment of the wider doctrine on Life in Christ only, (though often mistaken for the whole of it), and it is necessary to repeat that that wider doctrine is supported by several lines of evidence wholly distinct from the Scripture teaching on punishment. That this teaching agrees with the otherwise established truth of Conditional Immortality is, however, naturally regarded by us as a decisive argument in confirmation of it; and it is no small indication of its validity that it delivers us at once from the incredible horrors of the Augustinian theology, and from the ruinous mental and moral entanglements of Universalism.

AUGUSTINIANISM.

That every unregenerate human being, who, having been born in sin, has died in sin, is destined to an endless existence in some degree of misery of body or mind, or both—an existence, the duration of which would be *only commencing* when it had lasted through a number of millenniums denoted by lines of figures as numerous as the vibrating beams of light which extend from all the suns and stars of the firmament into the infinite darkness—even if these innumerable lines of figures should be multiplied into each other,—this is a proposition which requires for its support something more solid than a few disputed "texts" out of the English version of Matthew's and Mark's gospels, and which nothing short of absolute demonstration ought to persuade any man to embrace as from God. The more one knows of revelation as a whole, of the actual history of the human race, and of the character of God, as made known in the world that now is, and in the Bible, the greater is the difficulty in believing in this Augustinian doctrine of hell as Scriptural, and the deeper the conviction that the Deity of Augustine was, after all, only a fusion of the two eternal powers of good and evil of his earlier Manichean heresy.

UNIVERSALISM.

On the other hand it seems equally difficult to follow the Universalists to the opposite extreme, and to determine that the real meaning of a long series of revelations made by Almighty God through the prophets and apostles, (in which every term in Hebrew and Greek which can be used to denote utter destruction has been employed to convey the threatening of God's judgments hereafter on wicked men), is that all these wicked men are to be made heirs eventually of eternal life.   But the doctrine of conditional immortality causes no such shock either to our moral sense or to our common sense. It conforms not only to the laws of philology, but to the general laws of the physical and organic world, in which is found everywhere enormous " waste " of germs, disease leading to dissolution, and the survival only of the fittest ; and it agrees with the double representation made of the Divine Nature, in Creation and Revelation,—that while the Infinite Power is a Being of immense compassion and goodness towards those who observe His will, towards audacious law breakers, as science well knows, He acts with a severity which sets at defiance all modern sentimentalism on Father-hood, and ceases not but with their utter destruction.

MR. BROWN'S OBJECTIONS.

But Mr. Baldwin Brown contemplates this representation of the Divine Judgment as monstrous and incredible, and in this opinion we see that he is joined by Mr. J. G. Rogers. " The waste which it involves is too tremendous."   " Under this new version of the Gospel men are to be raised up and restored to life simply that they may endure anguish, so that God's wrath may find satisfaction in their torment." " A new horror is added to a doctrine which more than any single thing is respon-sible for the bitterness of the infidel hatred to the Gospel."

" Were it the only Gospel that man could listen to, it would, in time, make infidels of the human race." "It perpetuates in a new, and what professes to be a permanent, form, the incredible horrors of the mediæval belief, with apparent mitigations, which really exaggerate them, while it adds a new and darker doctrine of its own." "Life given for a time," adds Mr. Rogers, "solely for the infliction of suffering ! A succession of miracles is to be wrought for the simple purpose of punishing men for their sins. A miracle is first to be wrought to *raise from the dead the soul*, not naturally immortal, and then another miracle to give it a body fitted for the suffering of fire."

The maintainers of this doctrine of future retribution are subjected to two strangely contradictory attacks. Here we have men of the highest capacity objecting to it on account of its incredible terribleness ; and perhaps the next able objector will dismiss it, without further examination, because it "takes away all fear of future punishment from before the minds of mankind." The garbled indictment varies. Sometimes the doctrine is to be set aside because it is too terrible to be true that God should "annihilate " a sinner after "untold ages of torment ; " and sometimes it is a removal of all the sanctions of moral government, because no one will be afraid of being raised from the dead " only just to be reduced to nothingness again."

It is impossible to follow in these letters all the windings of an opposition which seems to think almost any weapon sanctified by the use to which it is turned, in assailing a doctrine so heartily disliked all round, and which indeed proved critical to many in causing the rejection of Christ when on earth. It was when He had taught distinctly in the great synagogue at Capernaum that men had not " life in themselves," that salvation meant " living for ever," and that living for ever means " not dying " in the plainest sense of the terms, and that this living for ever depended on the closest spiritual union with Him—that "many went back and walked no more with Him " (John vi. 26—66).

I shall now proceed to make some reflections on Mr. Brown's principal objection.

1. On the expressions of strong condemnation above cited from Mr. Baldwin Brown and Mr. Rogers, I have first of all to observe that the objection raised by them against the resurrection of the wicked in order to the judgment of destruction lies not against us in any special manner, but against Catholic Christendom.   All except convicted heretics have in every age believed in the resurrection of the just *and of the unjust* (Acts xxiv. 15).   Select what theory you think best as to the nature of that corporeity, but if you profess to abide by the doctrine of the Catholic Church you must allow that Christ's awful words are authoritative, that " they that have done evil shall come forth to the resurrection of damnation " (John v. 29).   The established belief of Christendom has been that the wicked so raised from the dead shall be cast " into everlasting fire," there to suffer throughout eternity.   Why has not Mr. Brown found time to deliver four lectures against that form of the doctrine of the resurrection of the ungodly ?   Why are all his eloquence, scorn, indignation, argument directed against those who are teaching exactly what Christendom maintains—the resurrection to judgment—minus the element of infinity in the infliction, which has already nearly " made infidels of the human race " ?

Who would believe that the words above quoted are those of two ecclesiastics who, until quite recently, have consented, by silence, to the " Declaration of Faith" of the Congregational Union (Article XIX.)—that, " *The bodies of the dead will be raised again*, and the Supreme Judge will divide the righteous from the wicked, will receive the righteous into life everlasting, but send away the wicked to everlasting punishment."   Surely it is not for Mr. Brown and Mr. Rogers, who have maintained for so many years a consenting silence to the sense put by orthodox churches on these words, to break forth into exclamations of horror against those who are teaching something much less incredible. *Quousque tandem !*

If, moreover, we are to take Mr. Brown's words "literally," the objection which he so vehemently expresses against us lies in a large measure also against his own view of future punishment. He distinctly says : "I look on and see through the vista of the future *pain like a searching fire,* eating into the heart of the ulcer of man's nature." "There are visions of agony before the sinner when the reality of the unseen world bursts upon him." Surely these purgatorial "pains" and "agonies" are of a "miraculous" nature, and if they are "*like a searching Jre,*" they give a view of the Divine benevolence which differs little from our view of the Divine severity.

WHAT SAITH THE SCRIPTURE?

2. But these questions are too solemn to permit of much use of the argument *ad hominem* in the controversy. Let me, therefore, say next, that what has been taught by us on this subject has been so taught simply and altogether in the fear of God, as the result of what we think to be honest interpretation of the *records of Revelation.* Not one word have I to say on the ground of reason, natural philosophy, or natural religion as to the results of human probation in a future state, before consulting Scripture. "Surely," (in the striking words of Mr. Thomas Walker, late editor of the *Daily News,* in a letter with which he recently favoured me,) "when the destiny of mankind is concerned, we cannot rest in the conclusions of speculative philosophy—too often the dictates of human pride —nor trust to the fancied results of psychological or historical analysis. We must have the assurances of our Father in heaven, which as men of faith we will accept. Far from us the

disposition to prescribe to the Divine Teacher, or to distinguish what he will find us ready to believe, *and that which we have resolved beforehand to reject.* Surely it must be the highest wisdom, humbly, thankfully, and unhesitatingly, to believe in the Son of God, who died to save us, when He speaks of the awful problems of human destiny."

Not one word, then, have we to say in defence of the doctrine of the resurrection of the wicked, and their destruction in the fire of God's wrath, unless these awful prospects are matters of Divine revelation which lie open to every eye. Why will the opponents persist in representing us as having invented this doctrine, and why do they persist in heaping contumely upon us as hard, bitter, and callous men, when there is so much more ready a way of ending the debate? Let it be shown and proved, not simply asserted, that the whole Bible ought to be read in the light of the assumed natural eternity of the soul of man. Let some rational explanation be given of the silence on this presupposed immortality of man, which characterises the entire record of Revelation. Let it be shown how it was that when the son of God appeared, He who was "the Word made flesh" always spoke in language whose natural obvious sense conveys the idea that He is the Giver of eternal life to mankind, if, in fact, man had this eternal life already in his own nature. And lastly, let it be shown why, in speaking of judgment to come on sinners, with one consent, all God's messengers, through all ages, have been directed habitually, scores of times, to use terms which signify in their obvious sense *one thing only*—namely, that all unregenerate men shall *die, perish,* and be *destroyed ;* shall be *burned up like chaff,* like *tares ;* shall be *dashed to pieces, ground to powder ;* shall *pass away,* with the Kosmos ; shall "*not see life ;*" shall be "*punished with everlasting destruction ;* " shall "*not inherit the kingdom of God ;* " when the truth was that after some beneficent chastisement they should "reign in life by Jesus Christ."

This process of putting an end to controversy ought not to

be a long one. If it is not a safe thing for men to read their New Testament until they have been well drilled in what the Rev. Mr. Rogers calls "natural religion," please to tell us what are its articles, and prove them. If it is not safe to read apostolic Greek in its natural sense, in the sense which its leading words bore in all other Greek literature, (in which to *die* means to die, to *perish* means to perish, to *pass away* means to pass away, to be *destroyed body and soul* signifies to be destroyed both body and soul), please to give us, by way of an Introduction to the apostles, for popular use, a sketch of the language as specially modified for the purpose of "Revelation."

Meantime, we are convinced that the statements which Mr. Baldwin Brown and Mr. Guinness Rogers denounce as so monstrous and incredible, are *precisely those which Christ, the Son of God, has affirmed,* which His apostles, Matthew; John, Peter, and Paul have repeated in every possible combination of terms —namely, that the wicked shall be "raised from the dead," shall "stand before God," shall be "judged according to their works," shall be "cast into everlasting fire," and in that fire shall "pay the penalty of everlasting destruction." (2 Thess. i.) Set aside those words of the messengers of God, and we have no further argument to offer to revolted Christendom. But so long as these stand unblotted from the New Testament, they who rest their faith on them will not cease to warn men to close their ears against the siren song of hypothetical Universalism, which must be luring men to their eternal ruin.

3. The truth, however, is, that for many ages the New Testament writings have been subjected by powerful parties to processes gravely called processes of interpretation, in which various human prepossessions and church interests have overpowered and perverted the testimony of God. Partly psychology, and partly what is called natural theology, and partly church tradition and superstition, have imposed their own senses upon the sacred writings, until the command-

ment of God is made of no effect. If men approach the Bible, already firmly convinced that "natural religion" teaches us the absurdity of any doctrine of a tripersonal God-head, or of the incarnation of the Divinity, or of an atonement for the sins of the world, or of the renewal of men by God's Spirit, of what avail is the united testimony of all the apostles in support of those revelations? The modern critical rack is equal to extracting any signification from those tortured witnesses. If, again, the Roman Church has resolved, for reasons of its own, on the primacy of Peter, and on the figment of the succession and supremacy of the Roman Bishops, why, by a due drilling in catechism and anathema for a thousand years, all Europe can be taught to "see" that interpretation of Revelation and Providence most clearly in the Scripture; and, indeed, in Papal countries it requires unusual grace and insight to see through the delusion. And so, if mistaking what I believe to be the God-inspired fear of "judgment to come," which is nearly universal in some form (even in the strange doctrine of the *Kormo* among the Buddhists, who utterly deny an eternal personality)—if, mistaking this fear of judgment for a proof of the soul's natural and absolute immortality, men approach the Bible deeply persuaded of the eternity of their own nature, the entire structure of Revelation, both in its silence and speech, fails to make known Him who is the Life of the world.

4. Yet since Mr. Brown and Mr. Rogers are sound Protestants, I put it to them, How would they endure it, supposing the question were on the personal Deity of Christ, and the atonement by His death, if when they had professed to ground their faith in these facts and doctrines on Divine revelation, and appealed, as they well might do, to the clear, explicit, repeated affirmations of Christ and all His apostles in attestation of them—how would they endure it if I, passing over the matter of direct and distinct Scripture teaching, persisted in

repeating some vague rationalistic objections to the Incarnation and to the Atonement, to the effect that such notions were a monstrous calumny on God's character, and a ready method of instilling atheism into the multitude? Would they not stead-fastly resist such a mode of attack as unfair and irrelevant, and persist in demanding a concentration of our attention on the questions: *Are not the New Testament writings a record of a Divine revelation?* and *Do they not teach these doctrines against which you revolt?* Now that is precisely our position. You will never overthow this teaching by sneers at "word-mongering." You must show that the threatening of "ever-lasting destruction" to a wicked man is consistent with his salvation.

The methods by which this is attempted by the advocates of Universalism are, I think, such as to assist, without designing it, the overthrow of faith in all revealed religion. No words ever can be depended on to signify anything, if the words in question here may signify universal restitution. You place the doctrine of the Incarnation, of the Atonement, of the Holy Spirit, in direst jeopardy. The violence offered by the Uni-tarians to the terms which teach these truths is not exceeded by yours. The Godhead of Christ and the Gospel of salvation must go down before such exegetical subversiveness. If Christ was the "Word made flesh," "His words are spirit, and they are life."

A CORRECTION.

5. I do not propose to discuss here the questions of detail which are always set in the front by those who incline to sub-stitute emotion for reasoning. Both Mr. Brown and Mr. Rogers speak of "torment for untold ages" as part of the doctrine of the "second death." It has not so been set forth by any one of the recent writers on this side within my ac-quaintance. For myself, in speaking of this awful mystery, I have endeavoured to keep strictly within Scripture limits,

and have affirmed nothing further than that there will be a
distinction between the doom of lesser and greater offenders,
"few " or " many stripes ; "—and that "Sodom and Gomorrha
are set forth as an *example* " of the judgment by " eternal fire."
The true and apostolic doctrine on future punishment is certainly one before which a man like Felix will "tremble," when
it is preached, as it ought to be preached, with reality, awe,
and tenderness. At the Universalist doctrine no man will
tremble, but every Felix will rejoice with exceeding joy. On
none of these points, however, shall I now dwell, because the
remainder of this letter must be devoted to some forgotten
principles which underlie the discussion.

THE BODY.

6. Mr. Baldwin Brown, in his zeal on behalf of the soul of
man, takes much less notice than the Bible does of man's body.
In Dr. Perowne's Hulsean Lectures it is shown, after the
Scripture and the ante-Nicene fathers, who were very strong on
this subject, how important a place the body fills in man's
constitution. Man is an integer, consisting of body and soul.
Neither of these elements alone is the man. This unity is the
direct subject of God's dealings both in mercy and judgment.
When God judged man at first, the humanity died. When He
would save man, the Word was " made flesh," and by the
suffering of death "abolished death." The Son of God "rose
from the dead," and all His servants are to rise after Him.
It is, then, only in accordance with God's dealings, if men
" receive in the body according to that they have done, whether
good *or evil.*" The real question is, Will God enter into
judgment with wicked men ? If He will, their appearance
before Him in corporal humanity is in accordance with the
nature of things. The body is the instrument for the educa-
tion of the mind and will, for the manifestation of the mind
and will, for the reward and punishment of the mind and will.
The infliction of Divine judgment on the body is in itself no

more incredible than its infliction on the spirit, and both are involved in retribution on the man. Suffering in a future world, which has been deserved, is at least as credible, under the government of God, as suffering in the present world which has not been deserved; and there has been not a little of that through the wickedness of mankind.

THE SPIRITUAL SOURCE OF UNIVERSALISM.

7. In reply to many fallacious consolations offered to impenitence, I must profess my persuasion that much of the religious teaching of the last few years has proceeded from a gradually-declining sense of sin in its evil, and in its deserts; as that again has proceeded from a declining sense of the justice of God. This is but to repeat the lesson of all history, that ages of great external civilisation, and of physical luxury and comfort, have ever been ages of epicurean theologising. Amidst plenty of corn and wine, amidst the illusions of art and beauty, men lose the sense of "the sinfulness of sin," of the righteousness and severity of God, and of the terribleness of the world of doom beyond. So is it to-day. "Men heap to themselves teachers, having itching ears." They will "not endure sound doctrine." Hell itself must become a school of glory; heaven the final refuge of a world of unfortunates, who really had almost every excuse for their villanies and crimes. Between the fall of Adam—and the force of circumstances— and the cheapness of vicious indulgences,—and the bias o heredity—and the difficulty of knowing whom to believe— Jesus or Mohammed, Paul or Rousseau, John or Voltaire—a hopeful case must be made out for every man; and if GOD Himself should "judge the world in righteousness," He must unsay all the ancient threats of exclusion from future blessedness; and, after some fatherly chastisement of "dogs, and sorcerers, and whoremongers, and murderers, and idolaters, and lovers and makers of lies," must receive them with open arms to paradise. This is certainly the tone of much of the

most fashionable preaching of our time, both in and out of the
National Church.

If I stood alone in this generation (instead of re-echoing the
judgment of myriads of the wisest and holiest men) I must
till death continue to raise an outcry of alarm to my fellow-
sinners against this sure sign of an approaching deluge.
Never has this tone taken possession of the Church, but some
dread era of judgment has vindicated the reality of the government of Him " whose feet are like fine brass burning in a
furnace." Oh, for the awful voice of some Savonarola to
thunder over the heads of the ungodly millions of Europe, and
awaken them to the realities of judgment to come; to turn
their attention away from the "prophets who prophesy smooth
things" to the true sayings of God. "The judge standeth
before the door," and here are the very signs of His approach
—men saying, Peace and safety!—all right, and all for the
best, in both worlds—when "sudden destruction is coming,
and *there shall be no remedy.*"

I wonder what the recent preachers of this Gospel of "love"
would have said if they had stood on high with Abraham, and
seen through the gloom the blue rain of burning sulphur
descending on Sodom and Gomorrah, inflicting a remediless
destruction on those unclean sinners against their own souls?
Would they have ventured on these bold philippics against the
Power that herein "confessed the failure of His earthly
providence," so that He "could do nothing else than kill off"
all that lived in the cities of the plain? Yet Christ declares
that even these Sodomites are to suffer *again* in the "resurrection of judgment," though not so grievously as the men at
Capernaum and Chorazin, who beheld and rejected the Light
of the World. I wonder what they would have said of the
uniformly fatherly and purgatorial action of Divine judgment,
if they had been present in Pharaoh's Court, when, in the
name of the Almighty Lord of Nature, insulted and denied by
ages of Egyptian idolatry and philosophy falsely so called,

Moses, with uplifted rod, stood forth and said, from the mouth
of God :—" Now will I stretch out My hand that I may smite
thee, and thy people, with pestilence, and *thou shalt be cut off
from the earth.* And in very deed for this cause have I made
thee stand, for to show in thee My power, and that My name
may be declared throughout all the earth " (Exod. ix. 16).
Should we have been invited to listen then to some lectures at
Memphis on the "cruelty, and hardness, and bitterness " of
those who taught that this God of Love was a God of awful
Justice too, and, come what might, would not be "mocked "
by His creatures, nor spare a stiff-necked infidel who set his
mouth against the heavens? I think that if even Jannes or
Jambres had essayed such comments, they would soon have
shrunk from the conflict, and their " folly would have been
made manifest to all men." There are circumstances in which
it is good for the world that God's messengers should be armed
with a forehead of adamant, like Jeremiah, when the object is
to warn men as with the blast of the trump of God against
approaching doom ; when the sense of God's moral government
has well-nigh died out under the soporifics and enchantments
of so evil a time ; and when men and women will say and do
the utmost wickedness, in assurance of being fortified at last
in death "by all the rites of the Catholic Church" or by all
the deadlier consolations of a Protestant scepticism. " Awake
to righteousness and sin not, for some have not the knowledge
of God ! "

We read in the Gospels of some unhappy spirits—the
demons who spake through the possessed—who anticipate, at
a " time " yet future, " torment," and " destruction," and who
prayed Christ not to send them down "to the abyss." Let
any one reflect on that indication of the unseen world of
judgment, and surely they will think twice before they encourage
men by a single word to regard the invisible realms as a region
into which rebels and fools may safely rush in hope of salvation. The very grace of the Gospel presupposes a "wrath to

come," and that indignation is spoken of also for those who reject the Gospel, as " the wrath of the Lamb."

It is the burden of the Lord, and I feel my own unfitness to use the language of exhortation to Mr. Baldwin Brown; but my heart is so filled with the conviction of the truth and urgency of this argument that he must " suffer " it even from me, and not set down to malice what springs, I think, from conscience towards God and Humanity. If it was a good work to delve for seven days through the darkness and to cleave the rocks, to save those imprisoned miners from death in time, it seems to us as if it were for infinitely a nobler end to struggle through the long years of this fearful contention, in the endeavour to reach mankind sitting in death-shade, with the pure light of Life Eternal; for " he that hath the Son hath the life, and he that hath not the Son hath not the life."

In my concluding letter, I will consider the general bearings of this doctrine on popular faith, and especially on its alleged tendency to encourage speculative atheism and materialism.

LETTER IV.

THE substance of a large portion of the argument against attributing Immortality to Redemption, and not to the constitution of man's nature, is briefly this—that however harmless may be the influence of this doctrine on those who are already Christian believers, its external effect on the world at large will be immensely disastrous. It will degrade the whole conception of human life, by reducing human nature to the level of the animal races as to mortality, and will sweep away the two chief articles of natural religion, the stepping-stones of thought for faith in Revelation, namely, man's belief in his own spiritual being and relationship with a spiritual and eternal world, and therefore his belief in a spiritual and eternal God. It will aid all the existing materialism which speculates at present on the dependence of mind on brain, and thence will lead logically to a denial of the being of mind where brain does not exist ; even in Deity. In the thick darkness of the Atheism which this doctrine will shed over the earth all murderous and suicidal passions will hold sway, and the glory of man will be lost in a hell-smoke of infidelity.

On these charges I beg to observe, first, that it is an exceedingly mischievous and delusive method of procedure, in determining the meaning of the records of Revelation—a

4

method condemned by all past experience—to permit of speculation on the supposed *influence* of facts and doctrines, before deciding on their existence in the Bible. To permit such a method would be fatal to faith in Revelation altogether. Nearly all the prepossessions of mankind derived from an uninspired philosophy are hostile to the actual declarations o Christianity. " Eye hath not seen, nor ear heard," says St. Paul, " the things which God hath prepared for them that love Him. But God hath revealed them to us by His Spirit." " The world by wisdom knew " neither God nor Human Nature. Our first business, then, is interpretation and induction, not prophecy. The first question is, Are the prophets and apostles of Christ clear and unanimous on these topics ? We judge that they are ; but we think that we can show you that none of the threatened evil consequences of teaching this truth, which you anticipate, will occur.

OUR ADVANTAGE AGAINST MATERIALISM.

For first of all, the doctrine of immortality by recreation and resurrection meets, *on its own ground*, all the many-sided materialism existing in the world, and enables it to believe in God and a Gospel of Salvation. Mr. Brown evidently feels that, with his Gospel, he can do nothing for materialists. He must have a metaphysical battle with them first, and compel them to change their ideas on human nature, before he can persuade them to believe in Christ. Now that was not Apostolic Christianity; nor is it ours. The apostles evidently went forth with a Message which could save without delay Epicurean Materialists and Sadducees, without insisting first on a psychological conversion to faith in man's natural immortality and possession of a " never-dying soul."

This is precisely our position. We who hold this doctrine are not necessarily materialists. 7 myself am not one, but am strenuously opposed to that form of opinion. But the " Gospel which we preach " is adapted to meet, on their own grounds

—" just as they are "—materialists of every grade and type, with a moral certainty of a glorious result as to multitudes of them. Materialism is a creed which comprises many different ranks of capacity and respectability. There are the bad kinds of materialists, who have resolved that they are only a superior sort of organized animal matter, in order to give an air of philosophy to their much worse than brutal excesses. But there are also many far better types of materialism. You have the scientific materialists who are not atheists ; such as some of our noblest men of research and discovery ; and these hold ideas of Matter, as the effect of Energy, so exalted as to include within its possible combinations any degree of created intelligence, without resorting to the hypothesis of a second substance, such as Mind or Soul. With these thinkers Matter seems only another name for something like Spirit, so pure and so transcendent are their conceptions of its nature. Some of the most distinguished philosophers of past and present ages have adhered to this line of thought, without surrendering their faith in God as the Supreme and Everlasting Energy and Life of this universe. Of this opinion was Milton himself, as is proved both by the explicit argument of his book on the " Christian Doctrine," and by the following lines from the fifth book of the " Paradise Lost " :—

> " To whom the wingèd hierarch replied :
> Oh, Adam, one Almighty is, from whom
> All things proceed, and up to Him return,
> If not depraved from good, created all
> Such to perfection ; *one first matter all*
> *Endued with various forms, various degrees*
> *Of substance, and in things that live, of life.*
> But more refined, more spirituous and pure,
> As nearer to Him placed, or nearer tending,
> Each in their several active spheres assigned,
> *Till body up to spirit work, in bounds*
> *Proportioned to its kind.*—BK. v.

Of the same opinion still are not a few of the ablest thinkers in all parts of the world to-day,—theists they are, notwithstanding. Then next, there are the materialistic scientific and literary men, who are really Atheists also, but rather preferring to be called Agnostics than Atheists ; and some of them of a character so noble, so pure, so lovely, so sorrowfully sinking into the last and deepest abysses of doubt, that Religious Faith, instead of anathematising, must stretch forth a most loving hand to help their sinking souls before they die.

THE TRUE GOSPEL REACHES THE SADDUCEES.

Now the doctrine of life in Christ is a form of Christianity which is specially adapted to take hold of men who are thus convinced of the materiality of mind. It would be a poor thing if the Gospel had no word for those who were Sadducees, as well as for the Pharisees, if it could do naught to save men who are philosophical materialists; especially when we consider how tough and difficult an argument is required even from such men as Doctors Balfour Stewart, Tait, and Martineau, to beat out of their delusions a Mill, a Spencer, and a Tyndal. But we find it to be a matter of simple experience, that men of all intellectual grades, who, for one reason or another, have become theoretical materialists, and who, if abandoned to the influence of that philosophy alone, would be compelled to surrender all expectation of a future state for man, are drawn to faith in a future state, and faith in God as the Saviour in Christ, and faith in immortality by Resurrection ; so that numbers of these are being trained for the kingdom of heaven in a life truly spiritual. Christ, who is the Word made flesh, exerts a power which lifts them up to God, with a hope full of immortality.

Among these certainly must be reckoned the multitudes of Christian believers who have received the Gospel of Christ on our theological representation of it, but on a philosophical basis of materialism. Apart from Christianity, they would be materialists without a future. But see the effect of the teaching of Life by Christ and by Resurrection. These men, in masses, have become Christians. These Christian brethren have no faith in man's possession of a "soul" or "spirit," in the popular sense of the words. But they love life in its highest form, in God's likeness, and long for life eternal, and they have believed in Christ to salvation. Him they regard as the resurrection, and embrace Him with all their hearts. There are not a few prominent examples of such believers, led by the Spirit of God to Christ as the Life-Giver.

It has simply saved these men, as it is saving similar materialistic thinkers every day, who find this form of Christianity precisely adapted to meet their needs. And when I consider the difficulty and the complexity of the argument for a survival of the spirit, I am the less desirous of resting all the hopes of the world on such an obscure foundation; and tenaciously hold with Mr. Constable that the main object of faith is Resurrection by the power of Christ, reconstruction of the whole humanity by the Omnipotence of God. This is a basis of hope common to men of all opinions as to the nature of the thinking substance, and which invites alike the trust of spiritualists and materialists. Neither does it require much experience to show that not a few of these "materialistic" believers in Christ are among the most "spiritual" persons living on the earth—men of the purest lives, of the firmest faith in things unseen and eternal, of dauntless purpose, of heroic self-sacrifice, of devoted love to their Saviour, and of the tenderest sympathy to mankind. They live with Christ now, they think that in death their whole being will dissolve, but that Christ, whose members they are, is coming quickly "to create them anew, to immortalise and glorify them," and that they will have no sense of the interval between death and resurrection. I ask Mr. Brown if this can be called a brutalising result of the Doctrine of Conditional Immortality. Neither he nor I can prevent the wide diffusion in this day of scientific and semi-scientific materialism; there are millions who, led on by Spencer and Maudsley, will not listen to the old story of the Immortality of the Soul, and the more you preach it to them the more fiercely they revolt, and point to the phenomena of cerebral formation and cerebral decay; but to us it matters not, so much as to our opponents, how widely these ideas extend. We can preach a credible Christianity, and a present salvation to all materialists, high and low, by preaching to them Jesus and the Resurrection. *To this they will listen.* Their faith becomes an antidote to their philosophy, and they will, perhaps, some day learn to think differently on the one question which still divides us.

THE BEST ANTIDOTE TO MATERIALISM.

2. But we have a second answer to the charge of materialistic tendences, which goes deeper into the real causes of materialism. A perfectly logical materialism which, denying a spiritual basis of mind in man, denies it also in the universe, and enforces the result in a speculative positivism and atheism, may under certain circumstances become a real danger to society. It may corrupt the tone of popular feeling as to the moral dignity of man, and of popular faith as to his relations with an Unseen Deity. It is not we who have produced it.

But how may it best be encountered and overcome? My answer is, *not* by any simply metaphysical or philosophical process,—*not* by a psychology which may be riddled by the objections of Mr. Herbert Spencer, or made to look doubtful even by Mr. Holyoake. It cannot be checked even by lectures on the immortality of the soul, nor even by the additional bribe to faith of a promise of universal discipline and salvation. No ; the true remedy for a *debasing* materialism (for I will not admit that Milton's materialism was debasing) is to be found in the moral rather than in the intellectual realms of thought. It will be found, not in a contrary theory as to the substratum of mind, or as to the eternity of the thinking power, but in the preaching of a credible judgment to come, and of the grace of God in the salvation purchased by Christ.

THE SPIRITUALISING EFFECT OF GODLY FEAR.

If you wish to overcome the evil types of atheistic mate-rialism, you must awaken conscience, rather than entangle the intellect in doubtful disputations. Canon Mozley's discourse on *The Unspoken Judgment of Mankind*, in his "University Sermons," will do more to alarm atheistic materialists into repentance than the combined endeavours of my two friends at Brixton and Clapham to establish human hope on the basis of a metaphysical doctrine on the soul.

Men's philosophies spring from a great depth within them, from their spiritual states. Bid them, then, listen to the awful voice within, the utterance of a Will above the will, which persists in denouncing wrong and sin, and inspires an expec-tation of judgment. The liar, the thief, the fornicator, the adulterer, the murderer, knows in himself, when once awakened to solemn thought, that it is not incredible that there are con-sequences beyond—and consequences of the most tremendous character. These may be by survival or by the resurrection of damnation. Whatever makes these consequences appear credible, near, and certain, tends to awaken such reflections. Whatever removes the fear which an evil conscience inspires, whether it be an infinity of threatening, which generates un-belief, or the bold assurance of a general delivery from perdition at last, is so much gain for materialism. Whatever confirms the voice of the inward witness, and points to the "great white throne" of judgment, as the needle to the pole-star, is so much gain for a spiritual view of life and its belongings.

THE SPIRITUALISING INFLUENCES OF REDEEMING LOVE.

But this is not the complete answer. Christ is in every sense the Light of the world. His special message is not that

of Terror, but of Mercy. Proclaim that mercy. Preach the
Gospel to every creature. Bring near, with a heart that feels
it, the love of God to sinners. Set before them Christ "openly
crucified for them," "bearing their offences, carrying their
sorrows;" declare to the penitent the remission of their sins—
and you will wield against the bad sorts of materialism the
most powerful weapon in the world.

The true antidote to materialism is not found in a bold
ignoring of facts as to the generation of human nature, or as
to its structure and functions; much less in setting up a
metaphysic which confounds survival with eternal duration,
and even maintains survival of the soul by arguments which
revolt the judgment of many of the foremost philosophers of
the age. The true remedy is to overthrow materialism by
"saving" materialists, and this is precisely what the doctrine of
Redemption to Immortality by Resurrection especially enables
us to do. It presents Christianity to man's conscience, judgment, and affection, disentangled from theories which dissipate
its force by awakening scepticism rather than faith in the
hearers.

CONCLUSION.

Here, then, I shall make an end or answering Mr. Baldwin
Brown's criticisms on the doctrine to the promulgation of
which—not as a mere negation on retribution, not as a jejune
doctrine on "annihilation,"—not even as a positive doctrine on
the gift of eternal *being* (as Canon Liddon strangely misrepre-
sented it at St. Paul's Cathedral),—but as the gift of eternal
life, in God's holy image—I have devoted so many years of my
ministry. I am deeply sensible of the dangers which attend
controversy on things Divine; the danger of permitting the
idea contended for as God's truth to acquire a disproportionate
place in the sphere of daily thought; the danger of allowing
it to become separated from its organic and vital relationships
with all other truths; the danger of being blinded to those

important aspects of the same subjects which present themselves oftentimes in fullest force to opponents of the special
truth, which you may think that *they* have neglected, and you
are helping to rescue from oblivion; the danger, finally, of
permitting the dogmatic to swallow up the practical, and the
theological to poison the spiritual. If, in any of these respects,
we who have handled these awful themes of the life to come
have in past time offended, for such offence it becomes us to
ask forgiveness of God and of man. The last thing at which
we aim is to found a school, a party, a sect, or to lead away
disciples after us, or to set ourselves up as generals in an all-
reforming crusade. No humiliating recantation of error is
sought for on the part of Public Teachers. All we ask of
them is that they, and the teachers of the young, will cease to
speak in unbiblical phrase of "man's immortal soul," and then
the ideas that are in the air, and the words of Scripture, will
gradually effect the needed reform. With all my strength I
protest against every minister doing what some of us have
been compelled to do—making a public controversy on these
questions. The fewer controversies the better. What is
needed is not less practical fear of God's judgment, but more;
not a dispute on Heaven or Hell, but an embracing of Christ
as the Life of the world; and those are the best friends of
truth and of humanity who will make men feel most deeply
"the powers of the world to come."

I must again express, Mr. Editor, my thanks for the large
and liberal opportunity given for addressing these arguments
to English readers. If by any less guarded expressions in
these letters, I have given needless pain or offence to any,
I will not stand upon a word; and certainly towards Mr.
Baldwin Brown and Mr. Rogers, though so earnestly contending against their supposed deviation from the right line in this
department of theology, I can entertain no feeling except of
respect and good will.—I am, Sir, yours faithfully,

E W.

NOTE.

IN a former page I have invited attention to the doctrine of the gospel of John, and in order to assist the reader's judgment I subjoin a reprint of a criticism on the sixth chapter, which has been thought specially deserving of notice by competent judges. The reprint is taken from pp. 238-241 of my work on *Life in Christ*, second edition.

E. W.

SUPPLEMENT TO CHAPTER XVII. OF "LIFE IN CHRIST."

IT will be convenient to bring together in one view the indications afforded by this chapter of what we term the literal sense of *Life* and *Death* in our Lord's discourses, in opposition to the prevailing notion that *life* stands only for everlasting happiness, and *death* for endless misery. In examining the sixth chapter of S. John closely the reader is requested to bear in mind what the prevailing theory is—namely, that man's soul is immortal by nature,—so that all that comes to it from the hand of God, by the additions of judgment or mercy, is the *misery* or the *happiness* of a nature that is already eternal. The words of Christ on the donation of life, or the infliction of death, on this theory must therefore strictly signify the gift of *happiness* or the infliction of *misery*, and nothing beyond.

We propose to show that our Lord's statements in this chapter indicate that He meant much more than happiness or misery; He intended by life and death also, and primarily, immortality and destruction.

The discussion recorded took place in the great synagogue of

Capernaum, of which some interesting ruins yet remain at *Tel Hum;* for even the ruins are interesting of an edifice which was the scene of this notable revelation of Divine truth and grace.[1] The discourse was occasioned by the exclamation of Jesus, on seeing the people crowding around Him at Capernaum, after the miracle of Bethesda (ver. 26) : " Ye seek me because ye did eat of the loaves and were filled ! Work not for the food which perisheth ($\tau\grave{\eta}\nu$ $\dot{\alpha}\pi o\lambda\lambda\upsilon\mu\acute{\epsilon}\nu\eta\nu$), but for that food which endureth ($\mu\acute{\epsilon}\nu o\upsilon\sigma\alpha\nu$) unto Everlasting Life, *which the Son of man shall give unto you.*" The people, supposing that He offered to supply food which would confer perpetual life, ask, " What shall we do that we may work at the works of God ? " Jesus answered, " This is the *work* which God requires, that you should *believe* on Him whom he hath sent "—a work of the mind which would set all outward works right. " They said therefore, What sign showest Thou that we *may* see and believe Thee ? What dost *Thou* work ? Our fathers ate manna in the desert, as it is written, He gave them bread from heaven to eat." (Your gift of bread has been on the level of the earth, and only for a single meal ; can you not do something more like the miracle of Moses, who gave the whole nation food *from heaven* daily for forty years ? Unless you at least equal Moses, we cannot forsake him to believe in you.) " Then Jesus said to them, Verily, verily I say to you, It was not Moses who gave to you even *that* bread from heaven (it was God), but my Father now gives you the *true* bread from heaven. For the bread of God is He which comes down from heaven and gives *life to the world.* Then said they, Lord, always give to us this bread. And Jesus said, I am the bread of life. He that cometh to Me shall never hunger, and he that believeth on Me shall never thirst."

Now in this succession of sentences our Lord places together the idea of bread, as the *support of life*, and of Himself as the *giver of eternal life.* Bread is the aliment of life in the literal sense of the term. *Bread is not the symbol of happiness*, but of preservation of life, aliment for continued being.

---

[1] Canon Tristram mentions that on one of its remaining blocks of masonry, forming the keystone of the entrance arch inside, and therefore visible to the congregation, is sculptured the *pot of Manna*, the symbol of the God-given immortality.

This idea of bread as *the support of life* He then pursues to the end of the chapter ; and just as people who have no food must die so He teaches that preservation from death, and enjoyment of endless life, depend on receiving this heaven-sent aliment of being.

Ver. 41. "This is the will of Him that sent me, that every one which seeth the Son and believeth on Him may have *everlasting life :*" and in order to show that this life is not the *happiness of a soul* already immortal, but the literal life of a mortal being who consists of body and soul, He adds—"And *I will raise him up* at the last day." The Jews then murmured at His saying that He came down from heaven. He replied that their murmurings were vain, since none could come to Him unless attracted by the Father —and He then repeats it, "*I will raise Him up at the last day'* (ver. 44).

At verse 47 He returns to His first statement, and emphasises it again and again. "Verily, verily I say to you, He that believeth in me hath endless life. I am the bread of life." But now, in order to make still more clear His meaning as to to the sense of *life*, He brings into view the converse, *death;* "Your fathers did eat manna in the desert, and *died;* this is the bread that descended from heaven that any one might eat of it, *and not die.*" Here, then, Christ sets aside, once for all, every "figurative" sense of life and death, and shows by the contrast of the *literal death*, died by the manna-eating fathers, what was the signification of the life which comes with the bread of heaven. It consists in "*not dying.*" There is no nearer approach to a formal definition of terms in our Divine Saviour's teaching. It is inconceivable that such language as this would be used to denote the idea of a life which was only *happiness* or *spiritual character* given to a nature already immortal.

In verse 51 our Lord solemnly reiterates His doctrine. "I am the bread which came down from heaven. If any man eat of this bread he shall *live for ever*, and the bread which I will give is my flesh which I will give for the life of the world " (ὑπὲρ τῆς τοῦ κόσμου ζωῆς). Here is a steadfast adhesion to the idea of supporting the world's life, by food which is heaven-descended.

Verse 52. A natural exclamation follows : " How can this man give us His flesh to eat ?—Then Jesus said, Except ye eat the flesh of the Son of man and *drink His blood* ye have no life (not ἐν ὑμῖν, but ἐν ἑαυτοῖς) *in yourselves*. Whoso eateth my flesh and drinketh

my blood hath eternal life, and I will raise him up at the last day
For my flesh is truly food, and my blood is truly drink. He that
eateth my flesh and drinketh my blood dwelleth in me and I in
him." The demonstration of our Lord's meaning still unfolds.
Bread was the symbol of life ; but how much more was *blood*.
The blood is the life thereof," not merely the happiness of a living
being, but its life ; and here Christ declares that life eternal depends
on drinking His *blood*, which was His life. Under this metaphor
the main idea is clearly seen, and the metaphor is brought in to en-
force that idea. Man's literal life in eternity depends on receiving
Christ, and being united to Him. Apart from such union he will
" die."

At verse 57 a still loftier illustration is given of the intention of
the discourse. Our Lord defines the life spoken of by reference to
the life of God. "As the *Living Father* hath sent me—(not surely
the blessed Father or the holy Father, but the *ever-living self-ex-
isting, eternal* Father), and I *live by the Father*" (I derive my life—
my eternal *being*, in the way of dependence on the Original
Majesty),—" so he that eateth me, he also shall *live by me* ;"—shall
derive not merely happiness, but *being* from me, as I derive mine
as the only begotten Son of God, by generation from the Supreme
God.

Our Lord then enforces His idea of *life* by recurring, after this
lofty reference, to His former statement : "This is the bread that
descended from heaven ; not as your fathers ate manna *and died* ;
he that eateth of this bread shall *live to eternity*" (εἰς τὸν αἰῶνα).

The reader will judge, after thus examining this wonderful chapter,
whether it was possible for words to convey more distinctly to the
mind the statements,—

1. That man has no principle of eternally enduring life in himself ;

2. That God has given us eternal life in His Son ;

3. That man's actual enjoyment of eternal life depends on the
closest union with the Incarnate Life of God in Christ ;

4. That the eternal life bestowed on us includes and requires the
immortality of the whole humanity, and therefore carries with it the
resurrection of the dead.

The result of this discourse upon our Lord's hearers was to bring
to a crisis the inward revolt of many. "*From that time many of*

His disciples went away backward, and walked no more with Him.'
The doctrine of immortality through the Incarnation, and of death
eternal coming upon all men out of Christ, is the chief stumbling-
block of the gospel.   It was the last truth for the Church to learn
and the first for her to lose—as it will be the last that she will consent to receive again by unlearning the notion which makes man's
immortality independent of redemption.

The metaphorical part of this discourse, specially the difficulty
occasioned by His assertions of a descent from heaven, of the necessity of eating His flesh in order to eternal life, Christ at the close,
according to custom, explained to His faithful disciples.   "Are you
scandalised, said He—at my saying I came down from heaven?
What, then, if ye shall see the Son of man ascending where He was
before?"—a spectacle granted to them at Bethany.   And as to
" eating His flesh," that, He added, was a metaphor for receiving the
doctrine founded on the sacrifice of His flesh for the world's life.
" The flesh itself profiteth-nothing;" I'do not intend the literal eating
of my body.'   It is the truth respecting me which will give you
life.   " The *words* that I speak to you, they are Spirit, and they are
Life."   Whence we learn that by *life* our Lord intends precisely
what He says, " For it is the Spirit that giveth life " (2 Cor. iii.).

LETTERS TO THE "CHRISTIAN WORLD"
BY THE REV. S. MINTON, M.A.

INTRODUCTORY.

MR. WHITE, having expressed a wish that the following letters, which appeared in the *Christian World* after the publication of Mr. Baldwin's Brown's Lectures, in the year 1875, should be reprinted in conjunction with his own reply to more recent criticisms from the same quarter, I am very glad to append them. The lines traversed by the two answers, though leading to the same point, are so different that they may perhaps influence different classes of mind.

Not a word that I have heard or read since writing these letters has in the slightest degree, or for a single moment, shaken my fullest conviction, the strength of which I am wholly unable adequately to express, that they maintain, in substance the very truth of God's revelation. And I daily wonder, with ever increasing amazement, how any one—to use the words of a very leading man in the Irish Episcopal Church—"with two ideas in his head and a Bible in his hand, can doubt what its teaching is on this subject,"—when once the clue has been given him. It is an intellectual mystery, that utterly baffles my power of comprehension. Will any one try to find some single doctrine that is more plainly, positively, and constantly asserted, insisted upon, and illustrated, in every shape and form, from the beginning to the end of the Bible, than is the doctrine of Conditional Immortality? "This is THE RECORD, that God hath given unto us ETERNAL LIFE, and this life is IN HIS SON."

S. MINTON.

LETTER I.

Sir,—Every one must honour Mr. Baldwin Brown for the manliness with which he has spoken out his views, especially as it appears to have cost him a considerable effort. But, besides this, he has done the whole Church an immense service. I could have wished for a more courteous title to his sermons, and for the omission of a few expressions in the course of them: but which of us can see clearly enough to pull out these motes from our brother's eye? He is a man of like passions with ourselves, and I for one should be very unwilling, even. if he were not a personal friend of my own, to make him an offender for a word.

My chief complaint against him is that he did not state distinctly at first what just drops out very incidentally in the last sermon—that his severest strictures are directed, not against. the belief in conditional immortality (which is commonly understood by "annihilation"), but against certain views which are held by some of its advocates, and as strenuously opposed by others. Some years ago, when replying to an article in the *Contemporary*, I protested against the very same confusion of ideas; and, more recently, you did me the favour to publish two letters in which the protest was repeated against the prevailing habit of "miscellaneous hitting" on this subject. Now, my dear friend must excuse me for saying

5

that he has been striking out very wildly indeed. He candidly admits that what he contends against is not the living doctrine of immortality in Christ, but only its "skeleton," after he has cut away all the flesh from it, under the name of "padding"; a process which would give to Apollo himself a not very attractive appearance. But even into his skeleton he puts some abnormal bones, which are no more part of the system than Papal Infallibility is part of Christianity—held though it may be by a majority of Christians. And it is against those very excrescences that his fiercest indignation is launched.

For instance, he regards it as "blankly incredible" that the Son of God should have become incarnate in the form of "a highly developed brute," whom "a brickbat could put an end to." And he seems to think this an argument against conditional immortality. But some of us have long been contending, publicly and privately, as earnestly as Mr. Brown can do, against such views of man's nature. We consider the first part of our Lord's saying in Matthew x. 28 (" Fear not them which kill the body, but are not able to kill the soul") to be as decisive against those who hold the death of a human being to involve "utter loss of existence," as the latter part ("but rather fear Him who is able to destroy both body and soul in hell") is decisive against Mr. Brown. A brickbat cannot put an end to a man, but God can ; and, by telling us to "fear Him" on that account, Christ distinctly implies that in certain contingencies He will do so.

Again, a large part of Mr. Brown's denunciations (the word is used in no offensive sense) are grounded on the supposition that to believe in conditional immortality is to believe that every human being who is not brought to the knowledge of Christ in this life will be "swept into extinction." After saying, "The Church was once more pitiful," because "the bright gleam of hope suggested by the preaching to the spirits in prison was caught and cherished," he adds, "But these annihilationists are pitiless." The word "these" is manifestly collective, and not distinctive. Neither the title of the sermons, nor a single word that occurs till near the close of the last, gives the slightest indication of any distinction whatever existing in his mind. And yet, not to speak of my own letters addressed to yourself, the very first article in the current number of *Our Hope*, one of our organs which was strongly recommended not long since by the *Christian World*, is entirely occupied with enforcing the very suggestion which Mr. Brown says we are "pitiless" for refusing to "cherish"; and scarcely a number of the magazine ever appears without the same view being urged by some "annihilationist" or other. Two or three years ago a few of us spent a whole evening in examining that statement of St. Peter, and we were all agreed, with some minor shades of difference, that it was impossible fairly to put any other interpretation upon it.

This makes a very large hole indeed in Mr. Brown's indictment against the doctrine of immortality in Christ alone. Yet I am far from regretting that he has thus spoken; for I hope that it may enlarge the views of some of our friends, and point out the directions in which, if our doctrine does not require to be modified, our language may require to be more guarded.

A far greater benefit than that, however, will, I trust, result from the earnest appeal, with which he begins and ends, for perfect freedom of investigation. To that I say Amen with all my heart.

His cannonade of the popular belief in eternal evil cannot but do immense good. From the title given to his sermons, it might be thought that he feels less repugnance to the idea of a hopelessly depraved life being perpetuated for ever than to that of its being put an end to. But the explanation probably is that he sees the one to be falling and the other to be rising; and, as practically standing in the way of his own view, he dreads the younger antagonist more than the older. However that may be, he does proclaim war against eternal evil, and in that we heartily thank him for his aid.

So far I think that neither Mr. Brown nor, what is a great deal more, his most ardent admirers, will feel inclined to complain of the tone of my reply. If you will allow me in another letter to point out where I join issue with him, and how, in my judgment, he has failed to invalidate our reasoning, I hope we shall part as good friends as ever, though unable to see eye to eye.

LETTER II.

Sir,—In addition to other things for which we have to thank Mr. Baldwin Brown, is that of letting us know all that can be said against our belief from his side of the question. We have long known what could be urged from the other side ; and now we may feel perfectly certain that we have received the most tremendous volley which Universalism will ever be able to discharge against us. For a Universalist he undoubtedly is, in spite of the very fine distinction on the ground of which he repudiates the name. He begins by professing that he has no theory of restoration to offer, and ends by offering a very distinct one indeed—namely, that every human being will probably yield sooner or later to the power of the Cross and become reconciled to God. Why repudiate the name which simply and forcibly expresses this theory ? It seems to me that Euclid might as well have protested that he was no mathematician, and had no definite proposition of his own to make. Universalism will never find a more eloquent or powerful advocate.

Well, I have read every word of his sermons—some of them more than once ; and I have no hesitation in saying that our fundamental position is absolutely untouched by them. He has scarcely even attempted to grapple with our main arguments. Indeed, any one could see, by the way in which from

the very outset he entered a caveat against the question being
decided by the direct testimony of Scripture, that he felt
himself unable to meet them. He said we should " hear little
of particular texts," and he spoke slightingly of " criticism " as
applied to the subject. But the whole Bible is made up of
particular texts, and criticism is only a scholastic word for
searching the Scriptures. Mr. Brown is compelled to resort to
criticism himself pretty freely ; he has to instruct his hearers on
" the balanced methods of Hebrew expression " ; and he rests
his proof of man's necessary immortality almost entirely on one
particular text, which every one admits to be exceedingly difficult, and the meaning of which has always been hotly disputed.
None of the plain people, who are said to be quite competent
to understand this matter for themselves without the aid of
learned criticism, would ever imagine that our Lord's comment
on Jehovah declaring Himself to be the God of Abraham, Isaac,
and Jacob—" for (they) all live unto Him "—proves the necessary immortality of every human being ; but having, by a process of reasoning which deprives the original saying of all
significance, satisfied himself that it does so, he pronounces
this one doubtful text to be " utterly fatal to the theory of annihilation." How many texts, as plain and positive as human
language could make them, would be considered sufficient to
be " utterly fatal " to his own theory ? He does indeed asseit
that " in entire harmony with this demonstration of our Lord
is the whole witness of Scripture : the immortality of the human
soul is not formally taught as a dogma ; it is everywhere after
the manner of Scripture assumed as unquestionable." How it
can assume as unquestionable that which it positively contradicts
on almost every page, is somewhat hard to understand. He
might just as well have said that Scripture assumes the non-
existence of God as unquestionable. If there are two things
which it formally teaches as dogmas, they are—that there is a
God, and that He " only hath immortality " ; consequently,
that no creature can be immortal, except in the sense that God

will actually preserve him alive for ever. *More than sixteen hundred times is the human soul or spirit spoken of in Scripture, and never once is it called immortal, deathless, never dying, or anything of the kind.* Is it credible, on Mr. Brown's hypo thesis, that not one of the sacred writers should ever have dropped a single word to show that he regarded the human soul as unquestionably immortal? Is there a preacher in the whole world who believes that doctrine, and yet has never let any such expression fall from his lips, even by accident? Mr. Brown appeals to the "larger teaching of Scripture." But where will he find anything larger than that? And can such a fact be put out of court merely by saying that we are "very fond of counting texts"?

The simple question is, whether, according to the teaching of Scripture, every human being will necessarily live for ever, or not. And the longer I think of it, the more amazed I feel that any doubt could ever have arisen on the subject. To justify this expression of opinion at all adequately would require something like a quarter of the space that you have so profitably allotted to Mr. Brown's sermons; and though you have always been most generous to me, I fear that you would be inclined to kick against the infliction. If your constituency would only be kind enough to "read my book," or any of the pamphlets on this subject, that I have spent a small fortune in printing and advertising, I should be content to say nothing more; but, knowing the difficulty of inducing people to lay out sixpence on anything written in opposition to their own views, perhaps you will allow me just to reply as briefly as possible to the remarks made by Mr. Brown on two of the crucial words in this discussion—life and destruction.

Life is interpreted, in the usual orthodox way, to mean happiness—all that makes life worth possessing. But will any one tell us, in the name of common sense, and the laws of human language, why the word life, with eternal or everlasting prefixed to it, should mean something totally different from what is

meant by it with any other epithet prefixed? A short life, a
long life, a happy life, a wretched life, a useful life, and so on
through the whole dictionary: no one has the slightest doubt
as to the meaning of the word life in all these cases. Why
should there be any doubt as to its meaning when an eternal
or everlasting life is spoken of? If you say that a certain life
will last only for a year, and another person says, No, it will
last for ever, you are both speaking of the same thing. And
what is the difference between saying that any given person's
life will last for ever, and saying that he will have everlasting
life? Mr. Brown tries to escape from it by charging us with
making life to mean merely "existence"; and Mr. Spurgeon
calls it "a colourless existence." We do no such thing. A
marble statue has existence; and if it were preserved un-
injured for ever it would have eternal existence; but it would
not have eternal life. Some men are now leading a life of sin
and misery; if their lives were perpetuated for ever in that condition, they would lead an eternal life of sin and misery; but
they would have a great deal more than existence. What we
maintain is, that life means life—whether it lasts only for a
time or lasts for ever. And the reason why the promise of
everlasting life necessarily carries blessing with it is that God
has declared His purpose to reconcile all things to Himself by
Christ; so that those who live for ever must share in that
general reconciliation. If God be true, an everlasting life of
sin and misery is impossible. I will only add, that in Matt.
x. 39 our Lord describes the life to be saved or lost hereafter by
a word which no one pretends can possibly mean holiness or
happiness: "He that findeth his life shall lose it, and he that
loseth his life for My sake shall find it." Both the argument
and the word employed demonstrate that He is speaking of
physical life. If we save our lives here by unfaithfulness to
Christ, we shall lose them hereafter; if we are willing to sacrifice them here for His sake, we shall preserve them hereafter;
or, in Ezekiel's words, we shall "save our souls alive." The

only difference is that, while here we can only save or lose our bodily life, we shall hereafter save or lose the life of our whole being, body and soul.

Then as to destruction, which is so constantly threatened to the finally impenitent. Orthodoxy interprets it to mean the destruction of their happiness, Mr. Brown the destruction of their sinfulness. So that to destroy a man is according to one view to make him perfectly miserable, according to the other to make him perfectly holy. And this in the teeth of our Lord's precise definition of what it is that will be destroyed,—neither his happiness nor his sinfulness, but the component parts of his being, his body and his soul, the man himself. On the orthodox theory, the words should run, " Fear not them which have power to make the body miserable, but have no power to make the soul miserable ; but rather fear Him who has power to make them both miserable in hell." On the Universalist theory they should be, " Fear not them which can make the body holy, but cannot make the soul holy ; but rather fear them who can make them both holy in hell." This argument may possibly admit of some reply ; but it is surely not so "vapid" a one as to need no reply.

Or again, unless the various figures employed to represent the future destruction of the impenitent be utterly deceptive and misleading, there can be no room for question as to their verdict. Are our Lord's parables to be utterly ignored ? And if not, can any one believe that the tares are burnt up to turn them into wheat, or the bad fish thrown away in order to make them good fish ? When the Baptist said that the wheat would be gathered into the Lord's garner, but the chaff would be burnt up with unquenchable fire, could any one imagine that the chaff would ultimately reappear in the form of wheat and find its way into the garner ?

It would be easy to pursue this to any length. But I must forbear ; only asking permission for one more letter, on the moral aspects of the question.

LETTER III.

SIR,—I think Mr. Baldwin Brown would scarcely deny that it is on the moral aspect of the question he mainly rests his case.

"The larger teaching of Scripture" simply means the teaching of those particular texts which appear to support his own view. The natural meaning of a vastly larger number of texts cannot be their real meaning, because it would teach something "degrading to man and dishonouring to God." This is just the most difficult part of the subject to deal with concisely, because of its intimate connection with the great moral mystery —the permission of evil. The moment we attempt to grapple with any aspect of that portentous fact, we get enveloped in such a cloud of smoke that it is difficult to know where we are. But still I will endeavour, with the very limited space at my command, to show that the moral difficulties which our brother has raised are very far from sufficient to overthrow the plain and positive declarations of Holy Writ.

It certainly cannot be degrading to any creature, however exalted, to say that it must necessarily be for ever dependent upon the Creator for the continuance of its life, and that the same power which created can at any time destroy it. Does any one feel that man is being degraded when we sing of Jehovah, "He can create and He destroy"? Nay, can we

conceive of the Creator bringing any being into existence that
He could not put out of existence? I cannot; I believe
such a thing would be utterly impossible.

The only question, then, is, whether man would be degraded
by any single member of his race being actually put out of
existence. Surely Mr. Brown will admit that an affirmative
answer to this question would be about as tremendous a stretch
of human pride as could well be conceived. Immortality is
such a marvellous gift to be bestowed upon any creature that
it is hard enough to believe in it at all. But for a whole race of
beings to say they will feel degraded if any one of their number
is not allowed to live as long as the Creator Himself, must
surely be the *ne plus ultra* of self-exaltation. Mr. Brown
cannot mean this. But, then, what does he mean?

He is so undiscriminating in his allegations against " these
annihilationists," that he may perhaps refer to some views
which he supposes us to hold as to man's nature being reduced to the level of the brutes by his fall, and only restored
to its original condition in regeneration ; so that the regenerate
are a " caste of immortals " moving about amongst beings of
another order. If any one holds such a view, let him defend
it. For myself, I believe that every man's physical constitution remains to the day of his death exactly the same
in kind as it was created in Adam, though probably with a
considerable loss of its original power and beauty. The only
difference between one man and another is of a moral kind ;
and on that difference, whether it become unalterably fixed in
this life or the next, depend the issues of life and death.
What is there " degrading " in this? Mr. Brown may be
right or wrong in his severity to "saints" and tenderness to
"sinners," but he will not deny that there are such distinctions,
or that our Lord and His apostles make them to be of tremendous importance. The difference between wheat and tares,
between " the children of God and the children of the devil,"
is not one of " caste "; neither does it make the one to be

." mortals," and the other "immortals." They are both alike
mortal ; but those who have "counted themselves unworthy
of eternal life" will "perish," while those who have believed
in God's only begotten Son, and sought for immortality by
patient continuance in well doing, will "not be hurt of the
second death," for "if any man eat of this bread he shall live
for ever."

Well, then, if there is nothing in this " degrading to man,"
is there anything in it "dishonouring to God"? How? I
confess I am at a loss to conceive, except on the assumption
that the Creator must never withdraw from a creature any gift
that He has once bestowed upon it. But that would require
every animal to be immortal, or, at the very least, to be com-
pensated hereafter for its sufferings here. Mr. Brown speaks
of their life being a pleasure to them. To some of them it
is. But what are we to make of those animals whose lives few
of us would be willing to endure, even to obtain an eternity of
blessedness? If the intelligent, confiding, faithful, affectionate
dogs, whom fiends in human form have subjected to the
frightful agonies of vivisection, were gifted with our friend's
eloquence, they might declaim against the "pitilessness " of
those who would deny them immortality in as burning words
as any that he has used of those who, while overwhelmed with
gratitude for the marvellous gift of eternal life, which they
believe has been bestowed upon them in Christ, and deeply
sympathising with the groans of creation, can feel no confidence
that all their suffering brethren will sooner or later partake or
the same stupendous blessing.

But has not man a vastly higher nature than the brute?
Assuredly. And that tells tremendously against his prospect
of immortality, if he violate it. For, difficult as it is to conceive
of the Creator bestowing such a gift upon a creature that could
never know or love the Giver, it is infinitely more difficult to
conceive of His bestowing it on one who might, but would not,
love Him for it. Our friend hopes that this will never occur;

he trusts to the power of the Cross to bring every human being into loving harmony with the Creator. But he admits that the absolute "freedom of the human will" must render it uncertain. And that alone would require some limitation to be put upon the scope of those "particular texts," on which he mainly depends, and which, if taken alone, would undoubtedly lend him strong support. We go further, and maintain that other declarations of Holy Scripture, too numerous to be overlooked, as well as too plain and positive to be evaded, absolutely forbid us to understand this "larger teaching" in the extreme sense for which Universalists contend. They assert in every shape and form that some men never will yield to the power of the Cross; that they will "receive this grace of God in vain"; that the Gospel which proclaims it will prove to them "a savour of death unto death"; that it will become "impossible to renew them again unto repentance"; and that for them "there remaineth no more sacrifice for sin, but a certain fearful looking for of judgment and fiery indignation which shall devour the adversaries." To pronounce it "dishonouring to God" that such should perish, is to say, either that God dishonoured Himself by creating free agents liable to evil, or that, having created them, He is bound in honour to keep them alive for ever at any costs to Himself, to the universe, and to them. So far from their destruction being inconsistent with perfect love, it is only one manifestation of that love. To borrow the language of the Rev. Samuel Cox from his article in *Good Words*, "For those who *will* be evil, what greater mercy can be shown than that they should be destroyed out of their misery by the love from which they will not accept any higher boon?"

The amount and kind of mental or bodily suffering which will precede or accompany that destruction we may contentedly leave with the Judge of quick and dead. That it will be something very terrible, much more terrible in some cases than in others, neither reason nor the language of Scripture can permit us to doubt., But whatever may be the actual process by which the consuming fire of Divine wrath will devour the adversaries —and of that we can form not the slightest conception—we may be perfectly sure that there will be nothing in it to shock the deepest instincts of righteousness or love, but that the conscience of the whole universe will be satisfied, and all creation will say, Amen.

So likewise may we confidently trust God to wipe away the tears that may start to our eyes at the thought of those whom we loved, as long as there remained anything in them to love ; but it will not be the " doomsman's stroke " that causes our regret ; it will be that, through "judging themselves unworthy of eternal life," they sank to a depth of moral corruption which rendered that stroke inevitable. The reconciliation in Christ of all things that were created by Christ—" and without Him was not anything made that was made "—will be none the less "real" because countless forms of life have passed away for ever, some without immortality being placed within their reach, and some through refusing to accept it. All things will be none the less "very good" because many things once became so hopelessly bad as to necessitate their removal. The dark cloud of evil that had once been allowed to settle on creation will have been rolled away. And as eternity unfolds the ever-extending glory and happiness which have been evolved out of it, and which, unless the Creator loves evil for its own sake, could not possibly have been obtained in any other way, we shall be less and less inclined to ask, which now sometimes we can scarcely help doing, whether any conceivable result can be worth such a cost. Our lips will never falter as we exclaim, "Oh the depth of the riches, both of the wisdom and knowledge of God ! " nor shall we have to add from the bottom of a trembling heart, and in the perplexity of a bewildered intellect, "How unsearchable are His judgments, and His ways past finding out."

What is there "miserable" in this? Nothing, that I can see; nor, I believe, that my honoured friend can see. It is not the doctrine of conditional immortality that excites his "intense repugnance," but certain other doctrines, which he supposes to be connected with it, and which certainly are sometimes conjoined with it in a more or less definite form. Transubstantiation has been engrafted on the incarnation; but it would hardly be fair to make it a prominent feature, if not the main foundation, of an attack on "the miserable doctrine of incarnation." We hold that "mortal man" is offered immortality in Christ; and that this is the plain natural and intended meaning of "the record which God has given of His Son." We hold that "the crown of life" is a prize freely offered to us in Christ, to be sought for "by patient continuance in well doing," and if won to be cast at the feet of Him who purchased it for us with His own blood. A variety of answers may be given to the multitude of questions that naturally arise as to the practical consequences of this doctrine, each of which answers should be discussed on its own merits. But the doctrine itself should not be made responsible for any consequences except such as necessarily result from it. For myself, I am unable to see one that creates any moral difficulty in accepting what, after having for years considered everything that can be said on all sides of the question, still appears to me the undoubted consistent and most emphatic testimony of Holy Scripture.

. We are no more the "discoverers" of this truth than Luther was the discoverer of justification by faith. On the contrary, we have always declared that it was the prevalent, if not universal faith of the Church for the first two centuries; that it is taught in the writings of later "Fathers"; and that although, like many other truths, it was almost buried out of sight during the dark ages, it has never been without witnesses since the Bible itself was disentombed at the Reformation. Luther wrote: "I permit the Pope to make articles of faith for him-

self and his faithful—such as, that the soul is the substantial form
of the human body, that the soul is immortal, with all those
monstrous opinions to be found in the Roman Decretals." In
the Book of Common Prayer we ask, "that we may rise to
the life immortal," "that we may so pass though things
temporal as finally to lose not the things eternal;" and for
our Queen, that God may "crown her with immortality
in the world to come." Locke maintained that only "he who
doeth the will of God abideth for ever;" Milton expressed it
in the "Paradise Lost"; Olshausen, no mean scholar or
divine, so far from holding that the necessary immortality of
every human soul is "always assumed in Holy Scripture as unquestionable," declared that "the doctrine and the name are
alike unknown to the entire Bible;" Archbishop Whately
argued in his own pointed way that life means life, and death
means death, in the Bible as well as in any other book; Archbishop Thompson says, in his "Bampton Lectures," "Life to
the godless must be the beginning of destruction, since nothing
but God, and that which pleases Him, can permanently exist."
But time would fail to tell of Watson, of Foster, of Alford, with
a host of other divines, great and small, living and dead, in our
own and other lands, who, though neither individually nor
collectively infallible, have cast into the scale a weight of authority which can scarcely be neutralised by the remark that "very
clever men" can make Scripture say anything. Some of those
who are weak in this world may of late have been chosen to
popularise this doctrine in a way that, for more reasons than
one, would have been hardly possible to the great and the
learned. But in either case the only question is, whether the
doctrine be of God or not. "To the law and to the testimony;
if they speak not according to this word, it is because there is
no light in them."

www.ingramcontent.com/pod-product-compliance
Lightning Source LLC
Chambersburg PA
CBHW030002030726
47499CB00008B/2854